WORD GIRL™

WORD UP

STEVE YOUNG
COVER ARTIST

SHANNON WATTERS
EDITOR

ADAM STAFFARONI
ASSISTANT EDITOR

SPECIAL THANKS TO LYNNE KARPPI, DANIELLE GILLIS, AND GARY HYMOWITZ

ROSS RICHIE Chief Executive Officer • MATT GAGNON Editor-in-Chief • WES HARRIS VP-Publishing • LANCE KREITER VP-Licensing & Merchandising • PHIL BARBARO Director of Finance

BRYCE CARLSON Managing Editor • DAFNA PLEBAN Editor • SHANNON WATTERS Editor • ERIC HARBURN Assistant Editor • ADAM STAFFARONI Assistant Editor • CHRIS ROSA Assistant Editor

BRIAN LATIMER Lead Graphic Designer • STEPHANIE GONZAGA Graphic Designer • DEVIN FUNCHES Marketing & Sales Assistant • JASMINE AMIRI Operations Assistant

kaboom!
KABOOM-STUDIOS.COM

For information regarding the CPSIA on this printed material, call: (203) 595-3636 and provide reference #EAST – 418791. A catalog record of this book is available from OCLC and from the KABOOM! website, www.kaboom-studios.com, on the Librarians Page.

BOOM! Studios, 6310 San Vicente Boulevard, Suite 107, Los Angeles, CA 90048-5457. Printed in USA. First Printing. ISBN: 978-1-60886-680-9

THE HAM VAN MAKES THE MAN

Anita Serwacki
WRITER

Steve Young
ART

Ryan Young
COLORS

Steve Wands
LETTERS

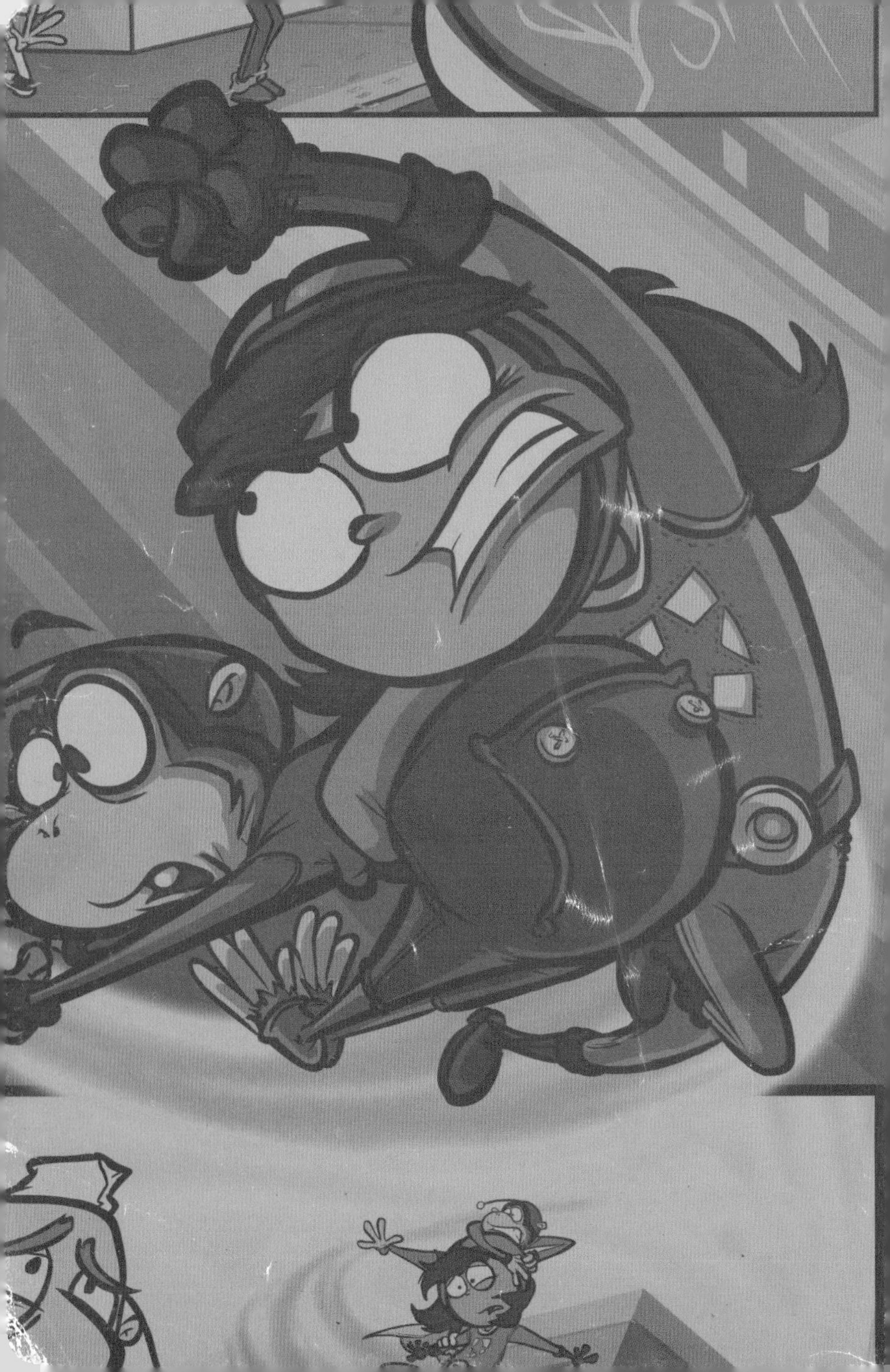

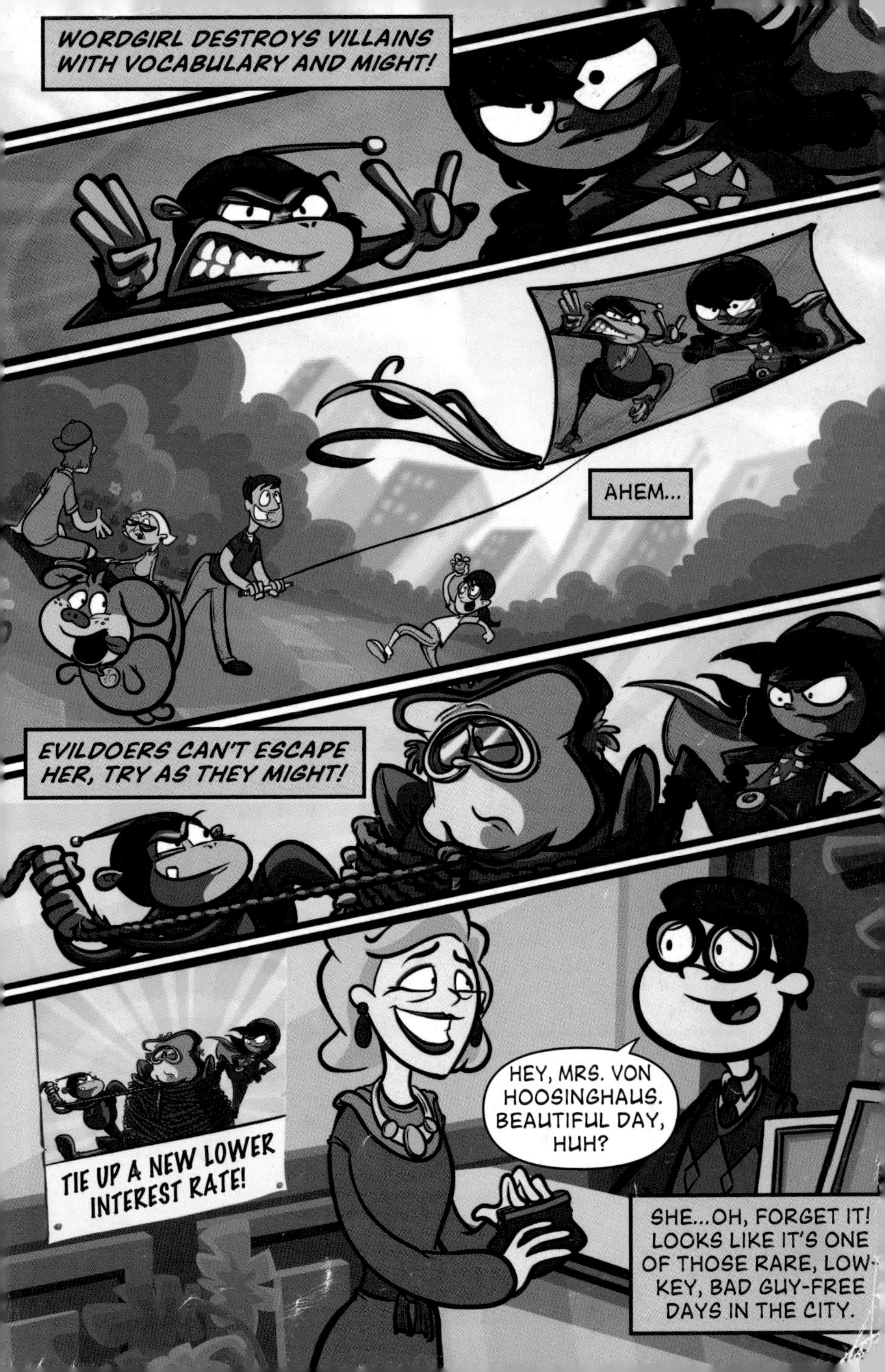
WORDGIRL DESTROYS VILLAINS WITH VOCABULARY AND MIGHT!
AHEM...
EVILDOERS CAN'T ESCAPE HER, TRY AS THEY MIGHT!
TIE UP A NEW LOWER INTEREST RATE!
HEY, MRS. VON HOOSINGHAUS. BEAUTIFUL DAY, HUH?
SHE...OH, FORGET IT! LOOKS LIKE IT'S ONE OF THOSE RARE, LOW-KEY, BAD GUY-FREE DAYS IN THE CITY.

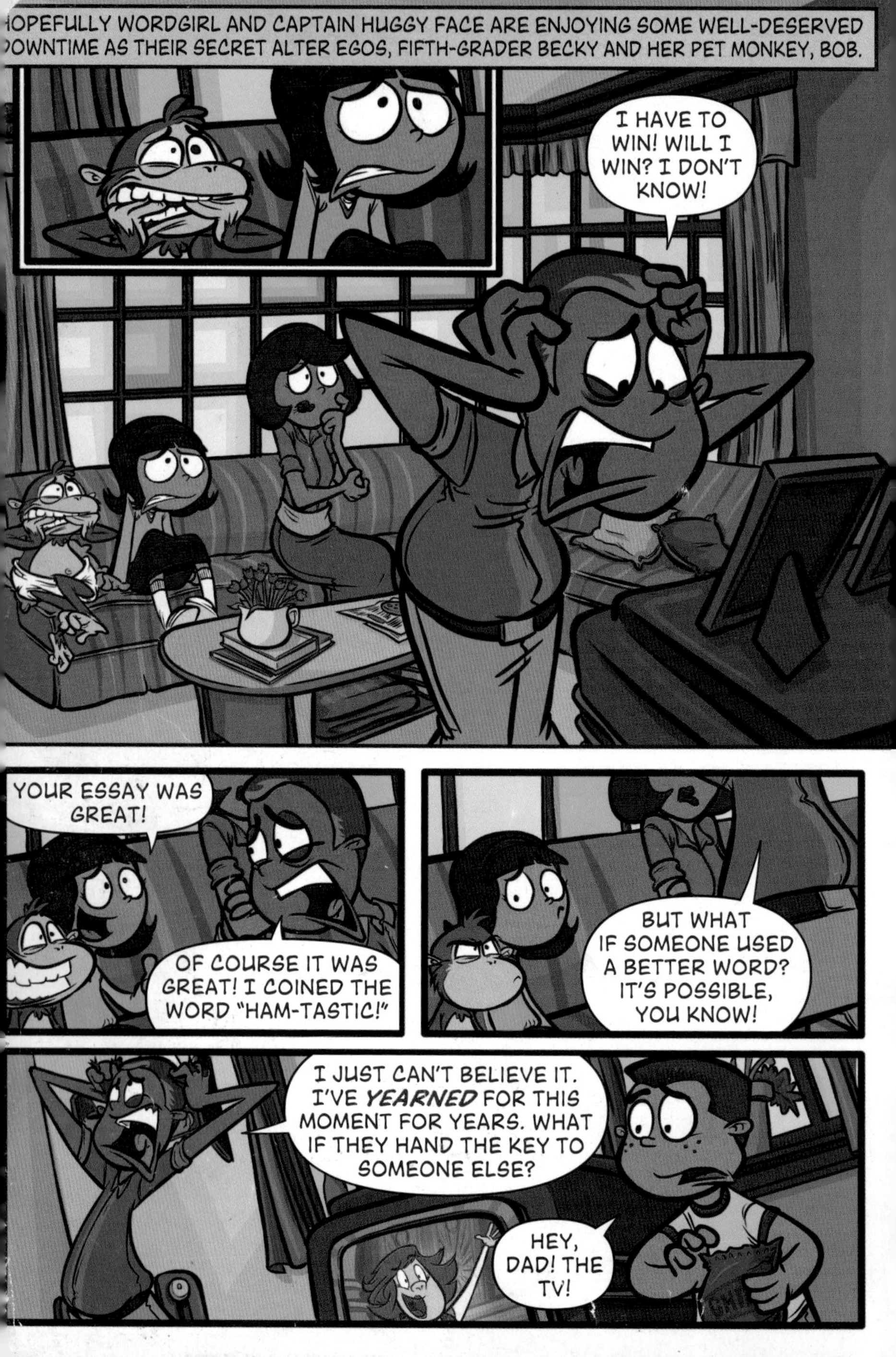

OPEFULLY WORDGIRL AND CAPTAIN HUGGY FACE ARE ENJOYING SOME WELL-DESERVED
OWNTIME AS THEIR SECRET ALTER EGOS, FIFTH-GRADER BECKY AND HER PET MONKEY, BOB.
I HAVE TO WIN! WILL I WIN? I DON'T KNOW!
YOUR ESSAY WAS GREAT!
OF COURSE IT WAS GREAT! I COINED THE WORD "HAM-TASTIC!"
BUT WHAT IF SOMEONE USED A BETTER WORD? IT'S POSSIBLE, YOU KNOW!
I JUST CAN'T BELIEVE IT. I'VE *YEARNED* FOR THIS MOMENT FOR YEARS. WHAT IF THEY HAND THE KEY TO SOMEONE ELSE?
HEY, DAD! THE TV!

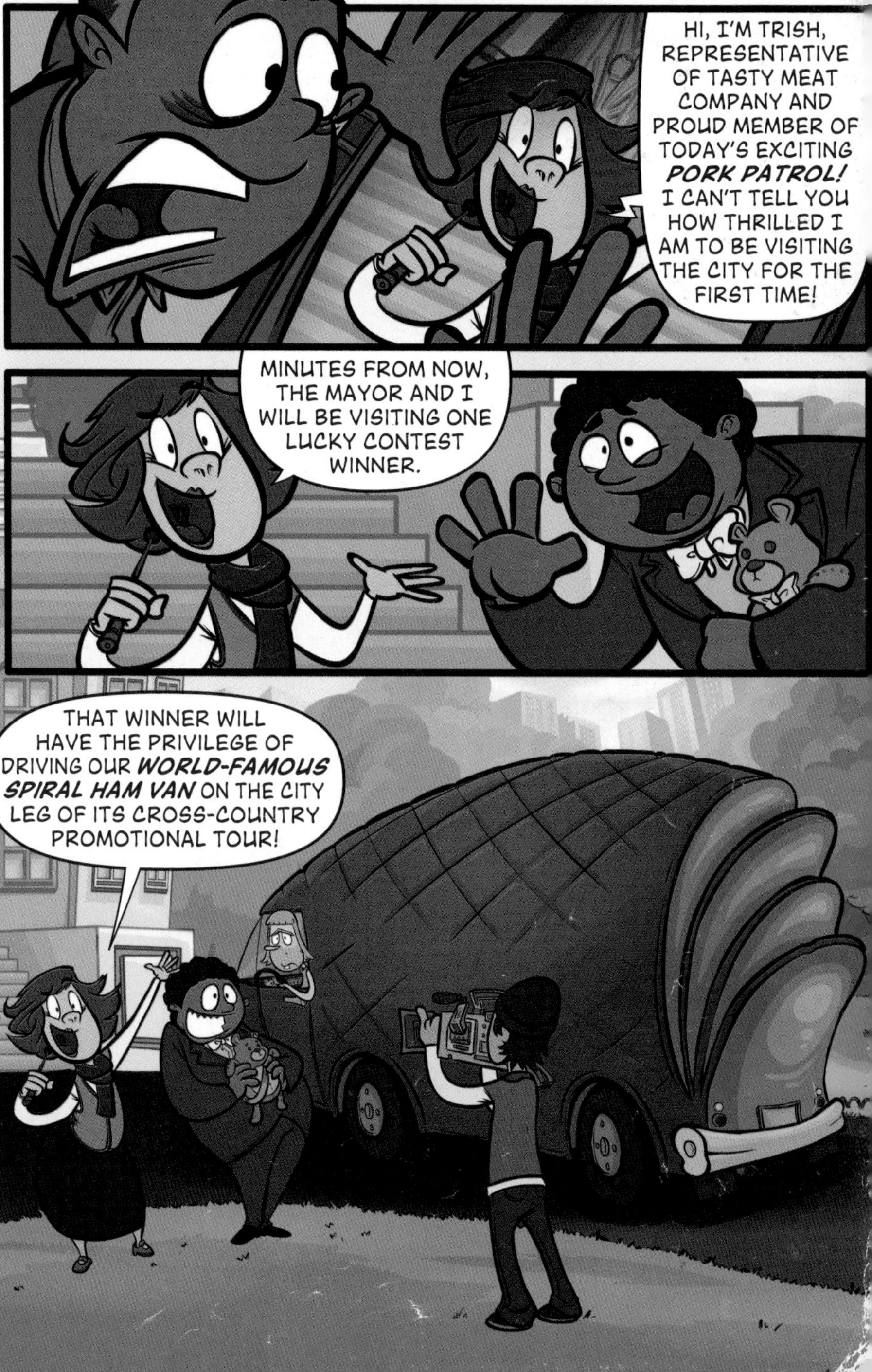
HI, I'M TRISH, REPRESENTATIVE OF TASTY MEAT COMPANY AND PROUD MEMBER OF TODAY'S EXCITING *PORK PATROL!* I CAN'T TELL YOU HOW THRILLED I AM TO BE VISITING THE CITY FOR THE FIRST TIME!
MINUTES FROM NOW, THE MAYOR AND I WILL BE VISITING ONE LUCKY CONTEST WINNER.
THAT WINNER WILL HAVE THE PRIVILEGE OF DRIVING OUR ***WORLD-FAMOUS SPIRAL HAM VAN*** ON THE CITY LEG OF ITS CROSS-COUNTRY PROMOTIONAL TOUR!

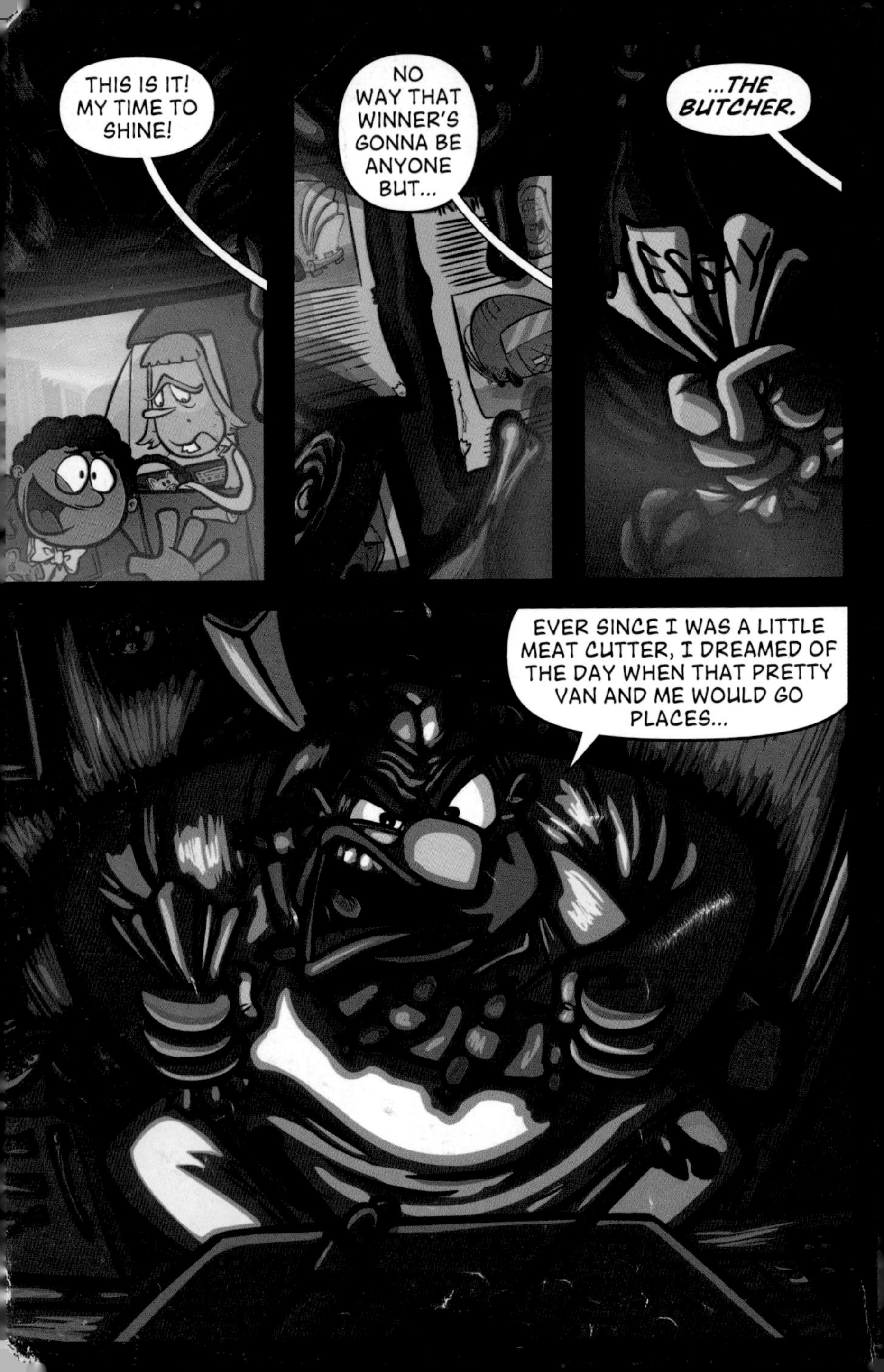
THIS IS IT! MY TIME TO SHINE!
NO WAY THAT WINNER'S GONNA BE ANYONE BUT...
...THE BUTCHER.
ESSAY
EVER SINCE I WAS A LITTLE MEAT CUTTER, I DREAMED OF THE DAY WHEN THAT PRETTY VAN AND ME WOULD GO PLACES...

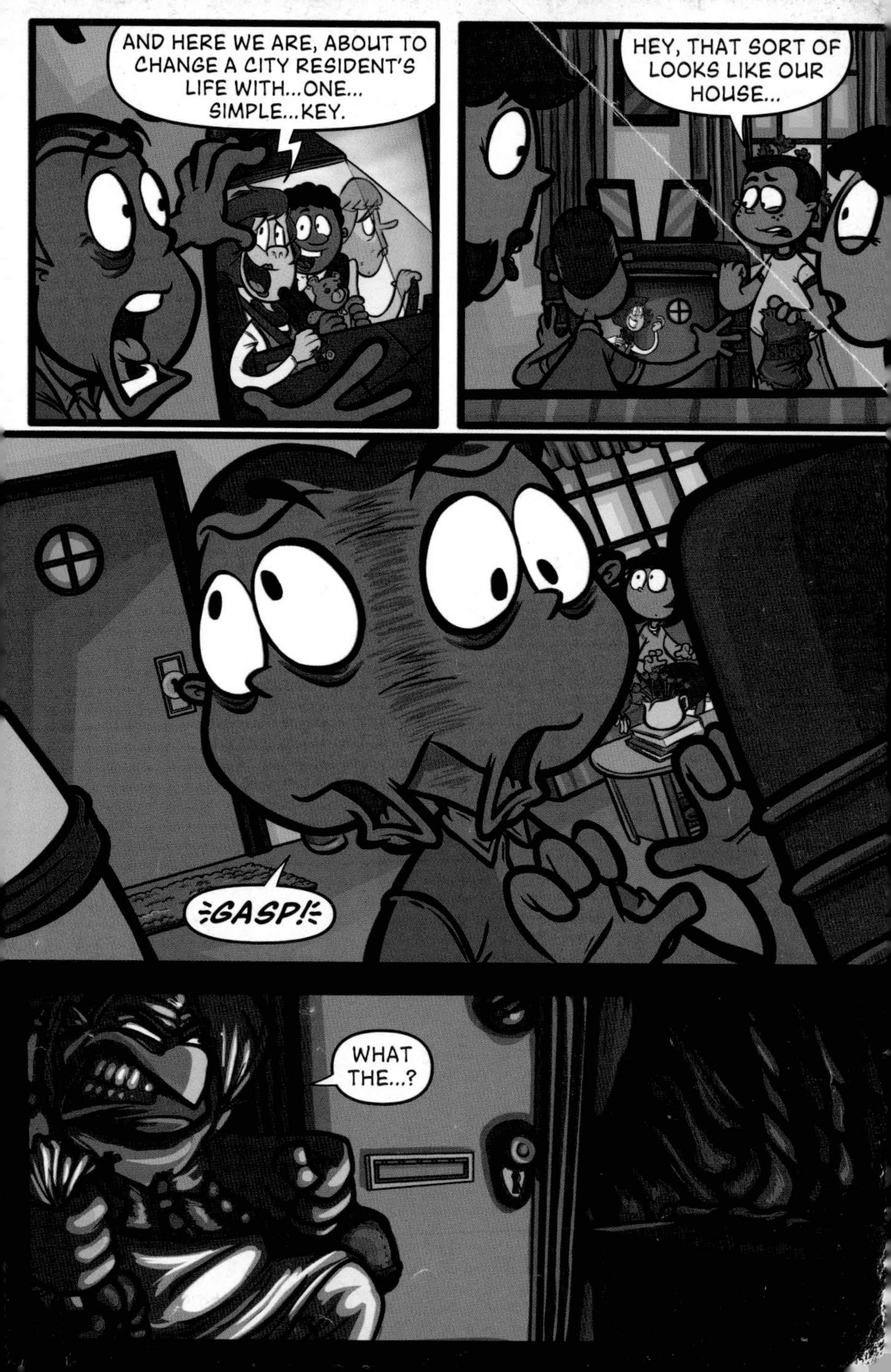
AND HERE WE ARE, ABOUT TO CHANGE A CITY RESIDENT'S LIFE WITH...ONE... SIMPLE...KEY.
HEY, THAT SORT OF LOOKS LIKE OUR HOUSE...
GASP!
WHAT THE...?

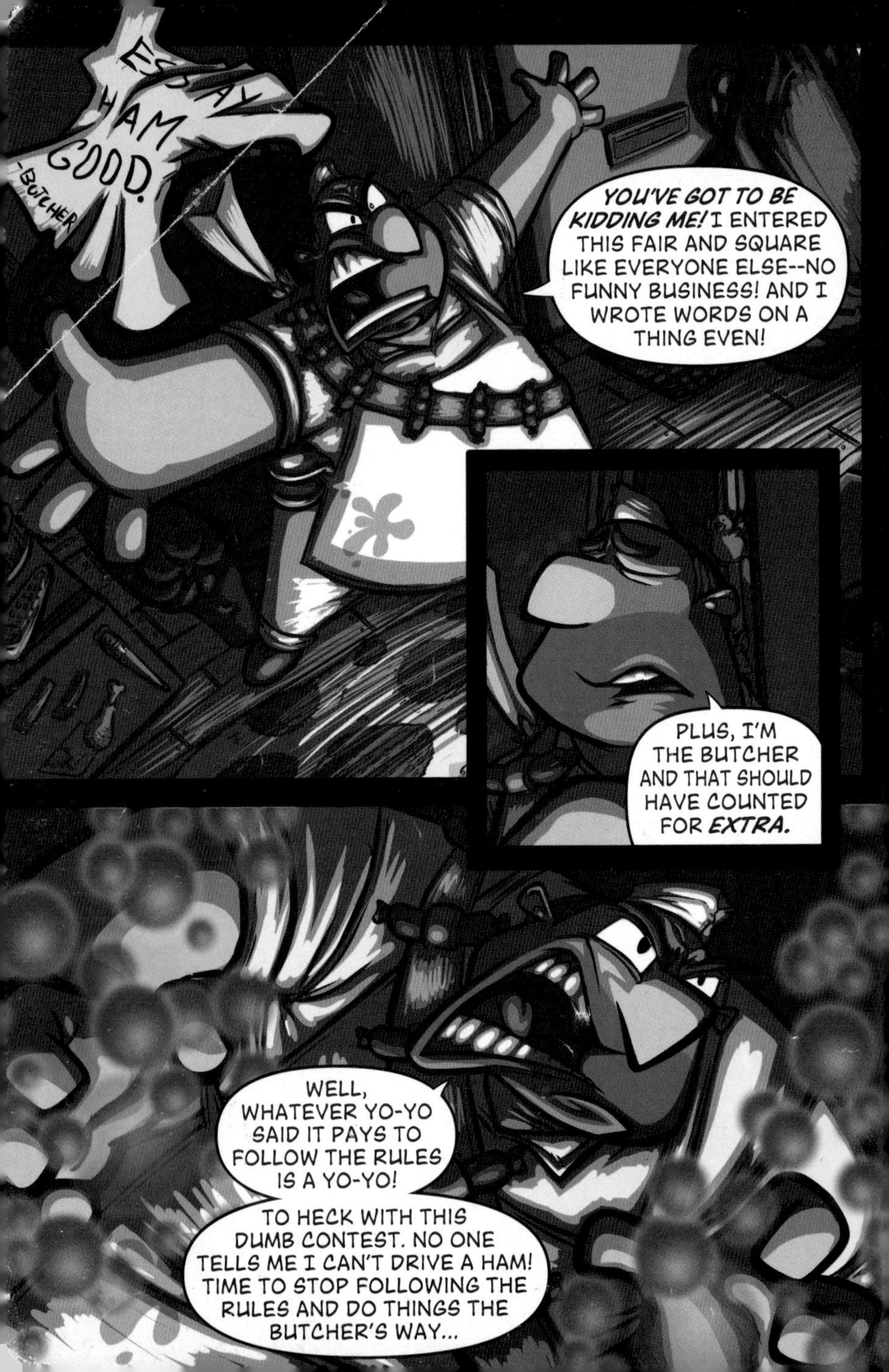
ESSAY
HAM GOOD.
-BUTCHER
YOU'VE GOT TO BE KIDDING ME! I ENTERED THIS FAIR AND SQUARE LIKE EVERYONE ELSE--NO FUNNY BUSINESS! AND I WROTE WORDS ON A THING EVEN!
PLUS, I'M THE BUTCHER AND THAT SHOULD HAVE COUNTED FOR *EXTRA.*
WELL, WHATEVER YO-YO SAID IT PAYS TO FOLLOW THE RULES IS A YO-YO!
TO HECK WITH THIS DUMB CONTEST. NO ONE TELLS ME I CAN'T DRIVE A HAM! TIME TO STOP FOLLOWING THE RULES AND DO THINGS THE BUTCHER'S WAY...

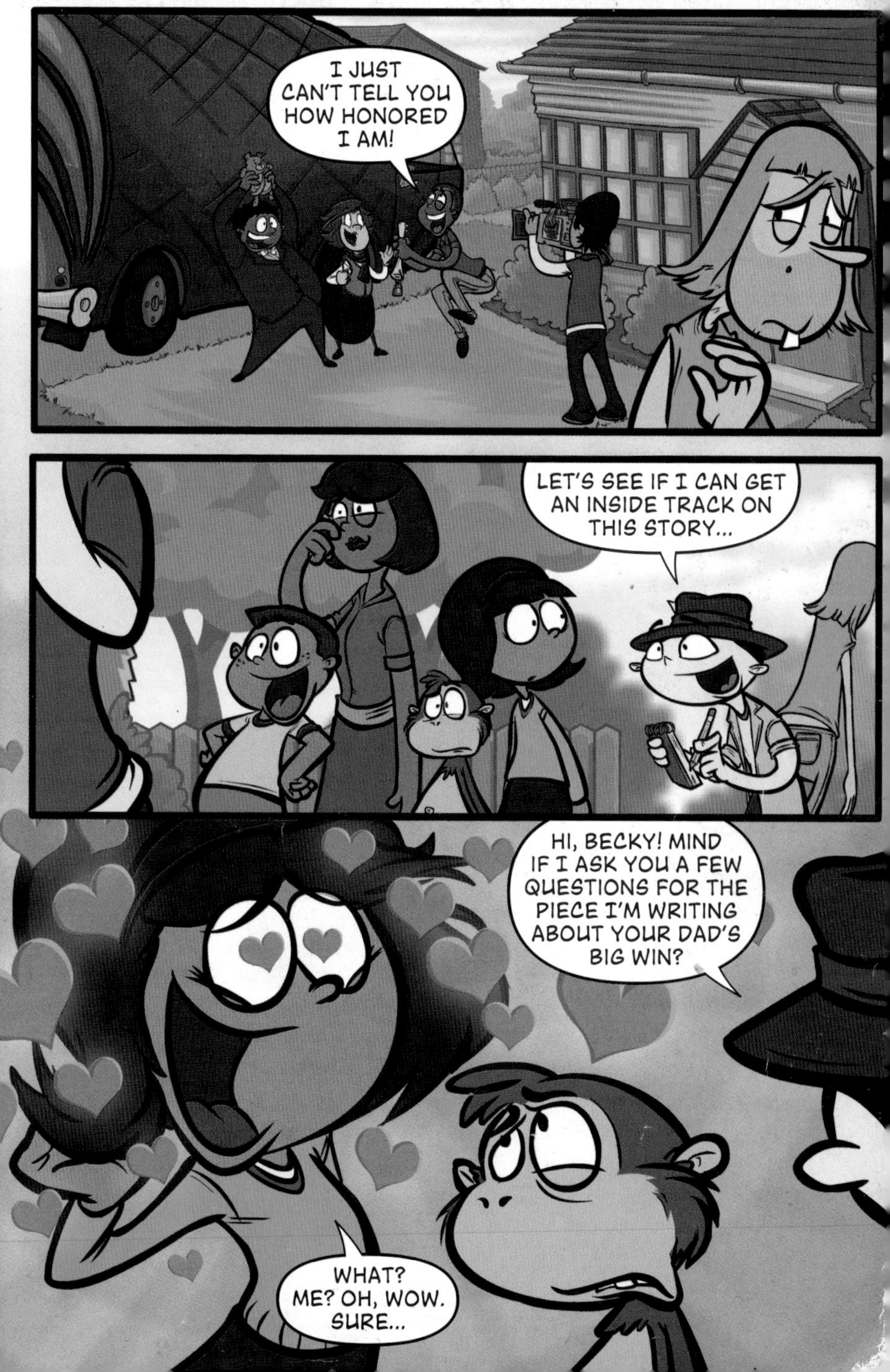
I JUST CAN'T TELL YOU HOW HONORED I AM!
LET'S SEE IF I CAN GET AN INSIDE TRACK ON THIS STORY...
HI, BECKY! MIND IF I ASK YOU A FEW QUESTIONS FOR THE PIECE I'M WRITING ABOUT YOUR DAD'S BIG WIN?
WHAT? ME? OH, WOW. SURE...

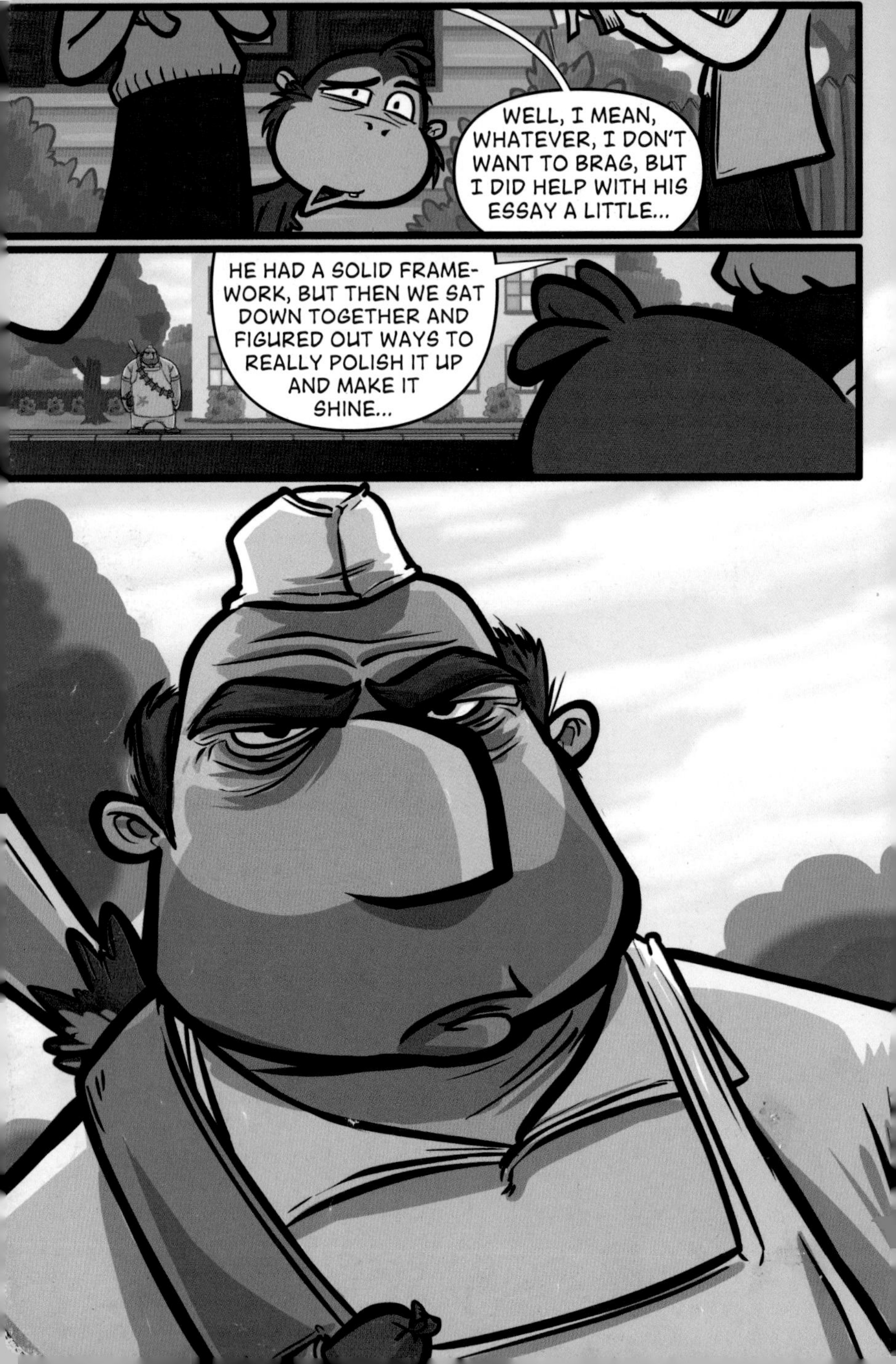
WELL, I MEAN, WHATEVER, I DON'T WANT TO BRAG, BUT I DID HELP WITH HIS ESSAY A LITTLE...
HE HAD A SOLID FRAME-WORK, BUT THEN WE SAT DOWN TOGETHER AND FIGURED OUT WAYS TO REALLY POLISH IT UP AND MAKE IT SHINE...

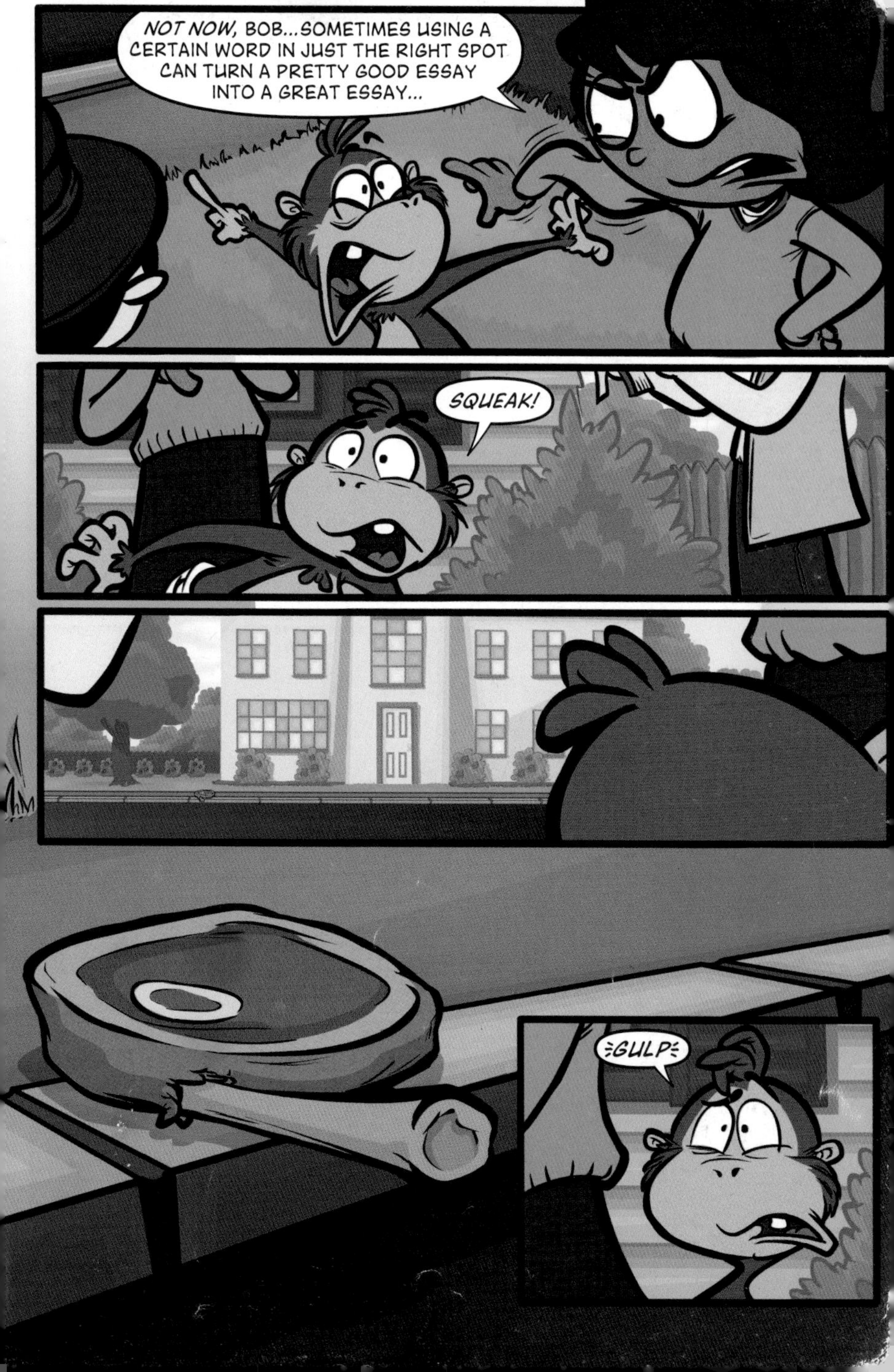
NOT NOW, BOB...SOMETIMES USING A CERTAIN WORD IN JUST THE RIGHT SPOT CAN TURN A PRETTY GOOD ESSAY INTO A GREAT ESSAY...
SQUEAK!
GULP

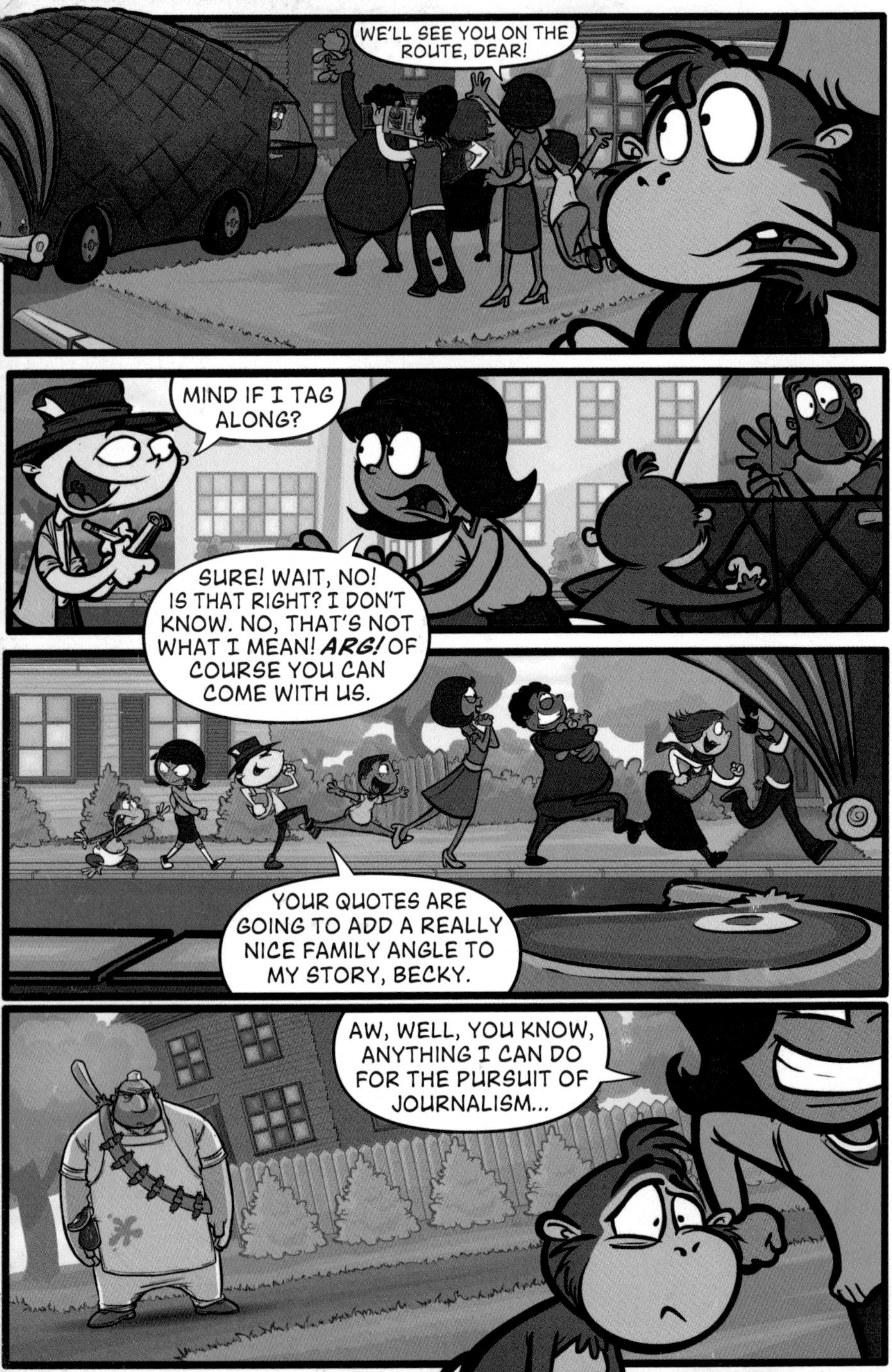
WE'LL SEE YOU ON THE ROUTE, DEAR!
MIND IF I TAG ALONG?
SURE! WAIT, NO! IS THAT RIGHT? I DON'T KNOW. NO, THAT'S NOT WHAT I MEAN! ARG! OF COURSE YOU CAN COME WITH US.
YOUR QUOTES ARE GOING TO ADD A REALLY NICE FAMILY ANGLE TO MY STORY, BECKY.
AW, WELL, YOU KNOW, ANYTHING I CAN DO FOR THE PURSUIT OF JOURNALISM...

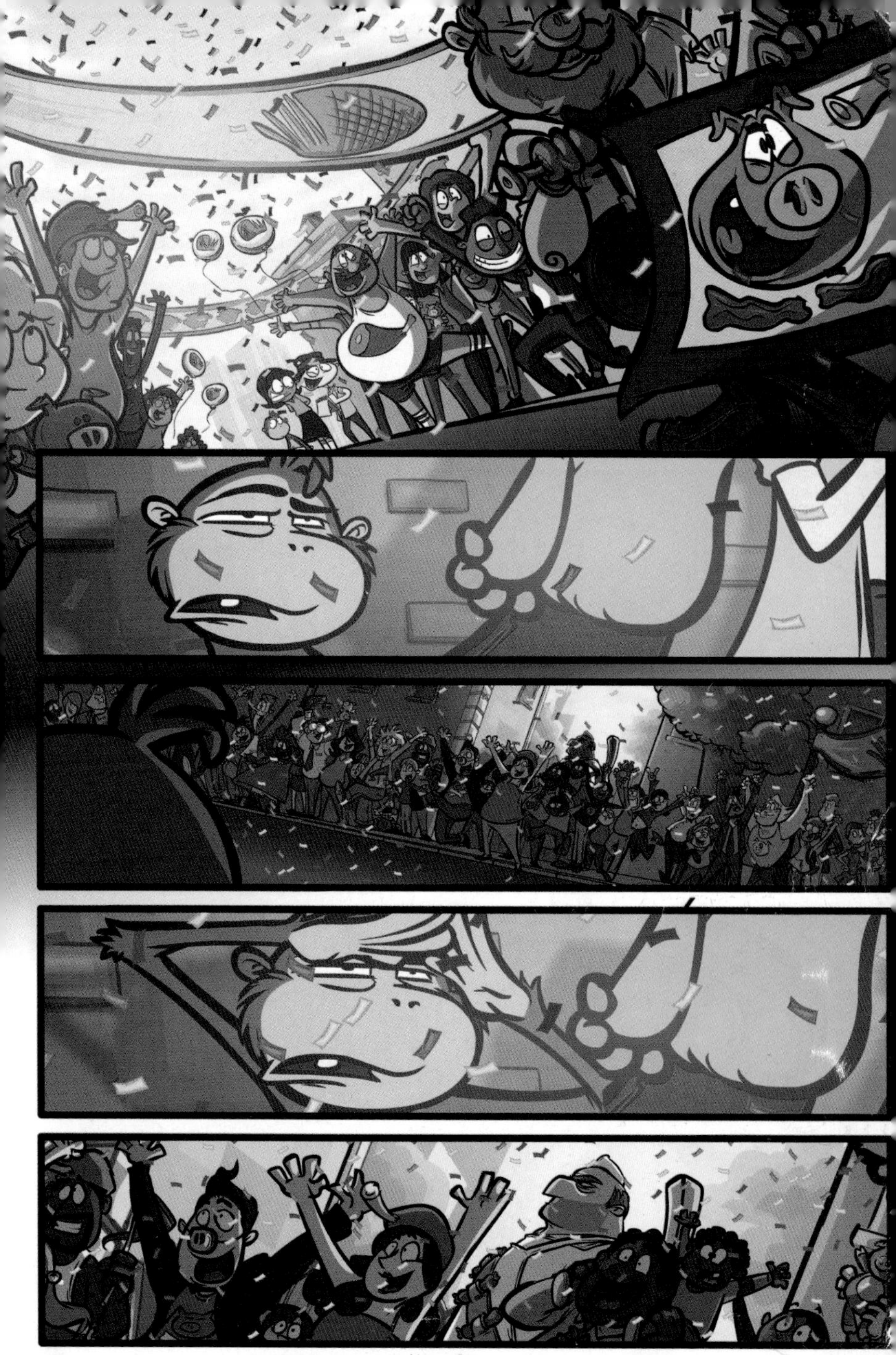

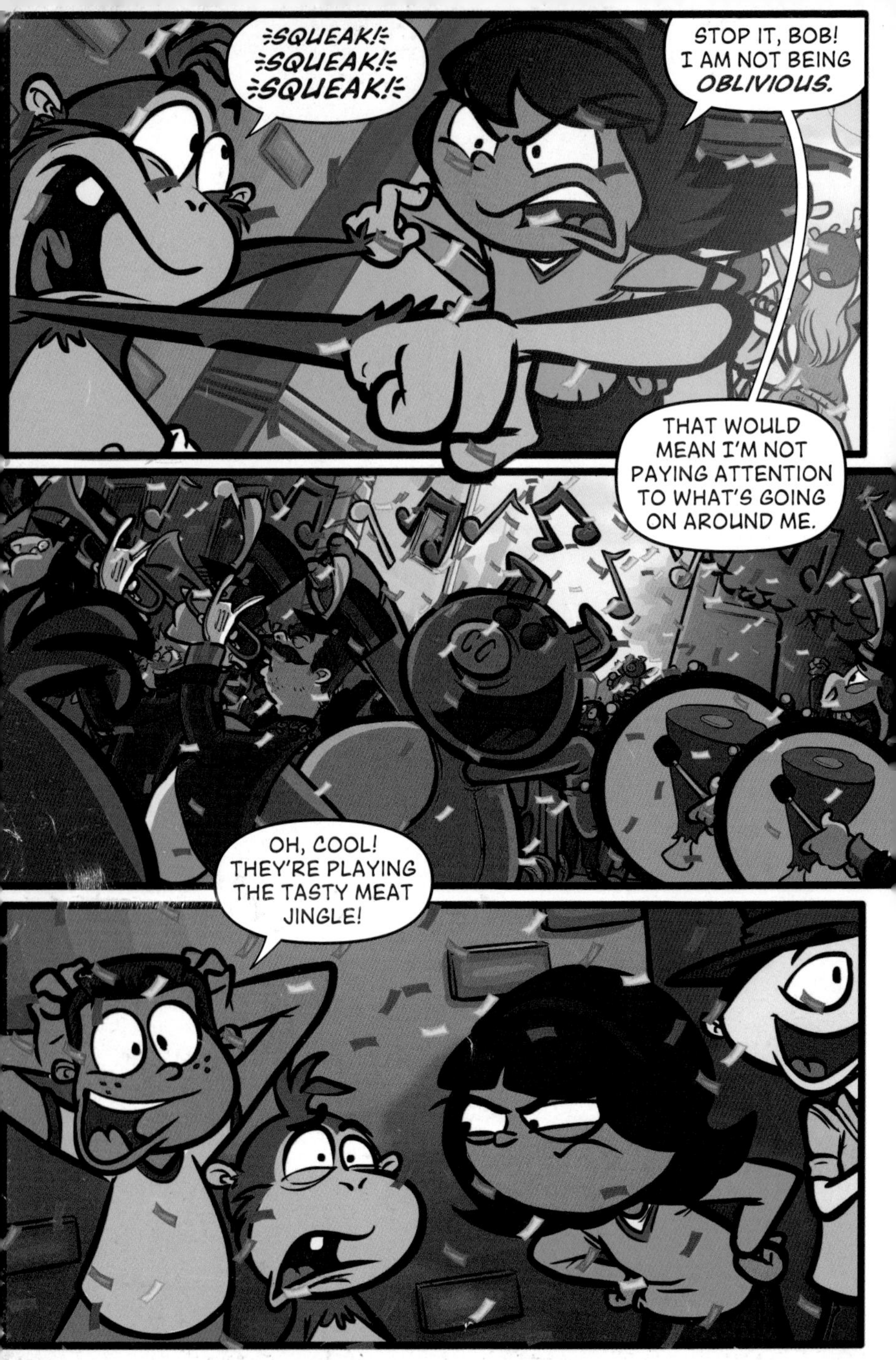

SQUEAK! SQUEAK! SQUEAK!
STOP IT, BOB! I AM NOT BEING *OBLIVIOUS.*
THAT WOULD MEAN I'M NOT PAYING ATTENTION TO WHAT'S GOING ON AROUND ME.
OH, COOL! THEY'RE PLAYING THE TASTY MEAT JINGLE!

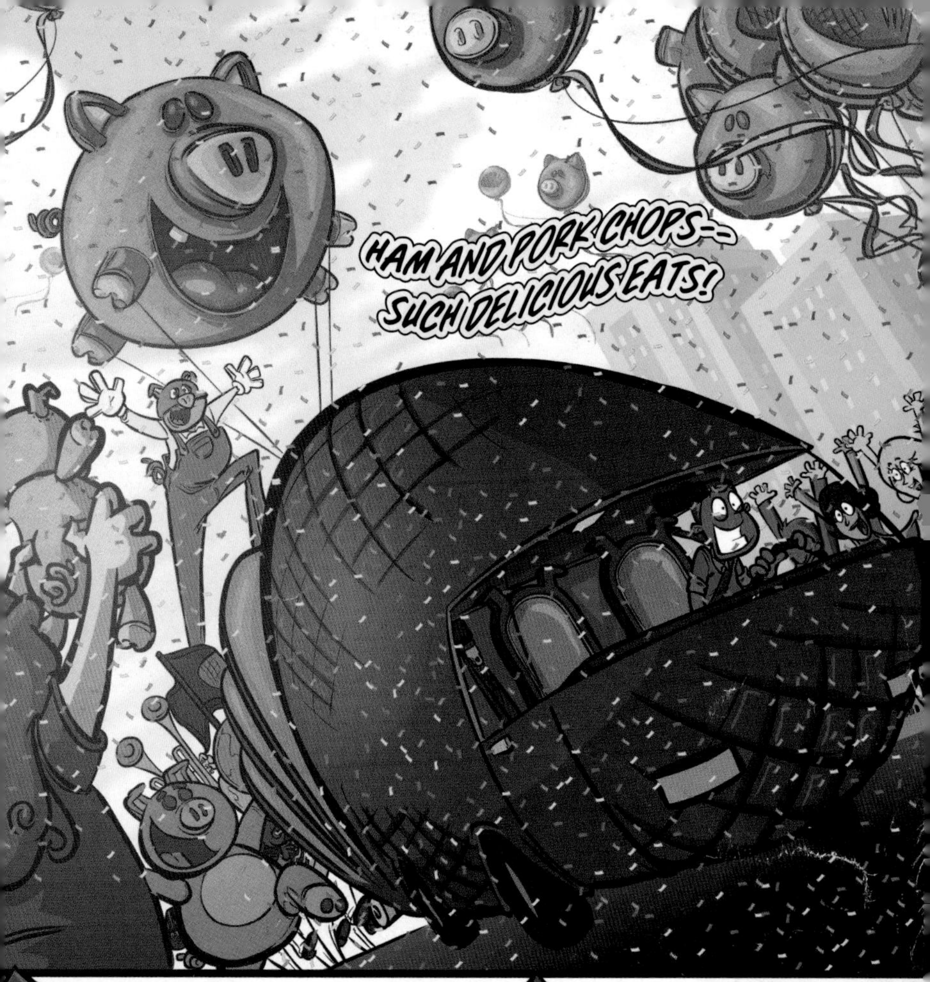
HAM AND PORK CHOPS--
SUCH DELICIOUS EATS!

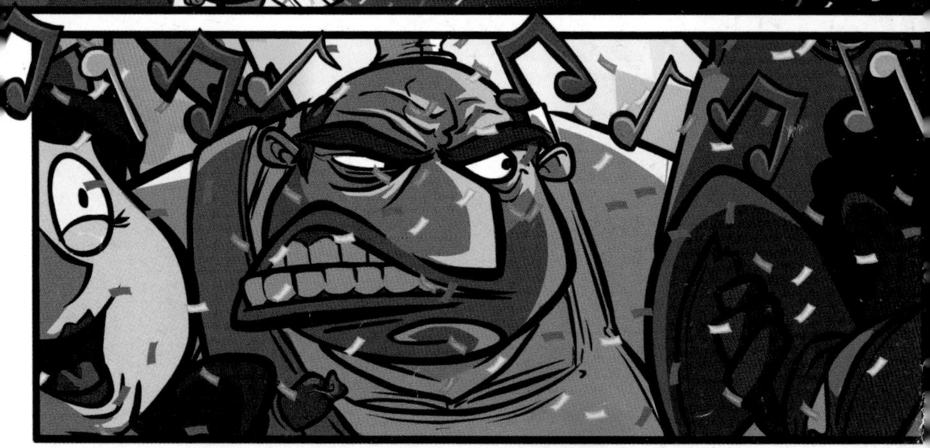

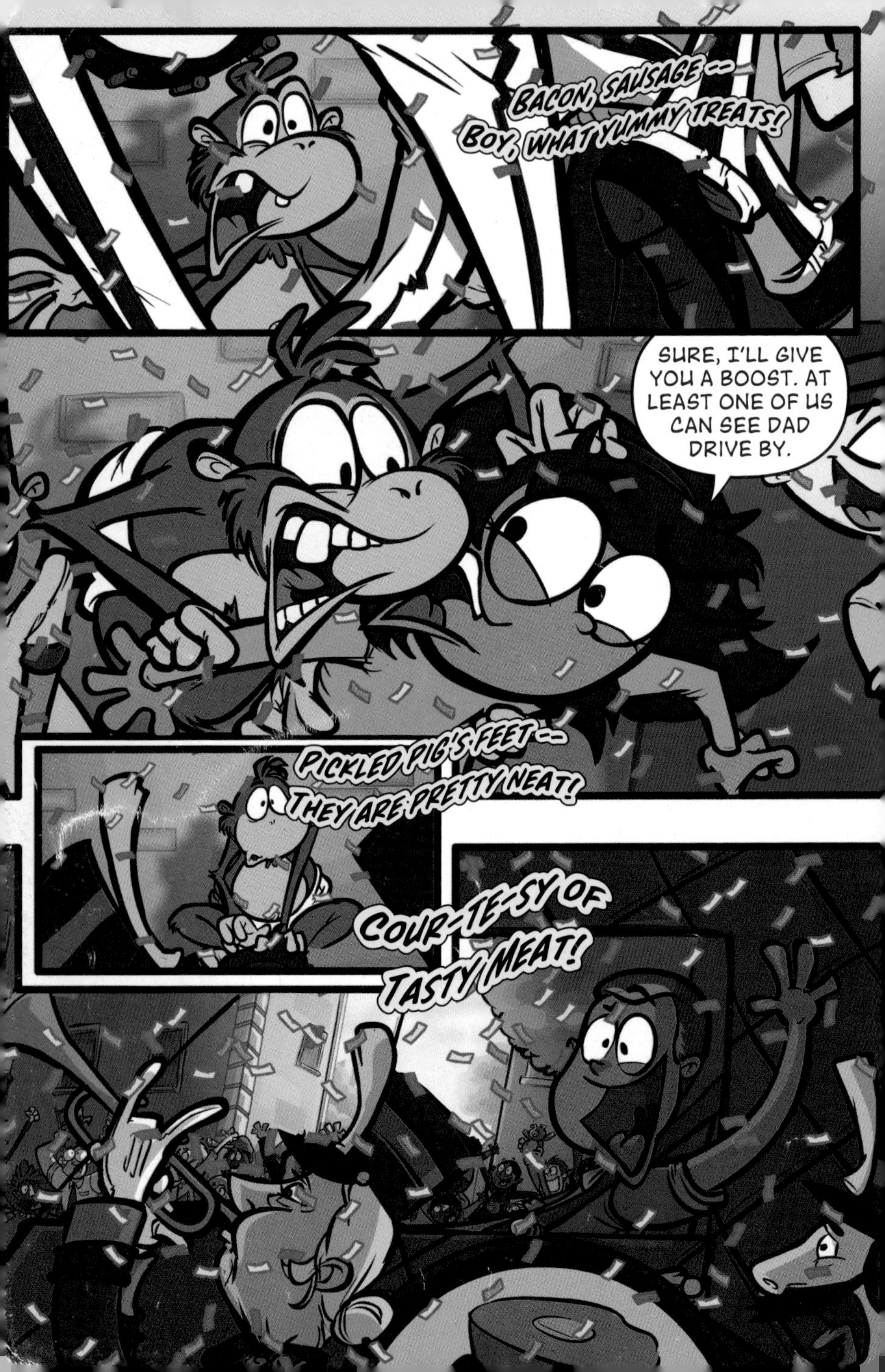
BACON, SAUSAGE --
BOY, WHAT YUMMY TREATS!
SURE, I'LL GIVE YOU A BOOST. AT LEAST ONE OF US CAN SEE DAD DRIVE BY.
PICKLED PIG'S FEET --
THEY ARE PRETTY NEAT!
COUR-TE-SY OF
TASTY MEAT!

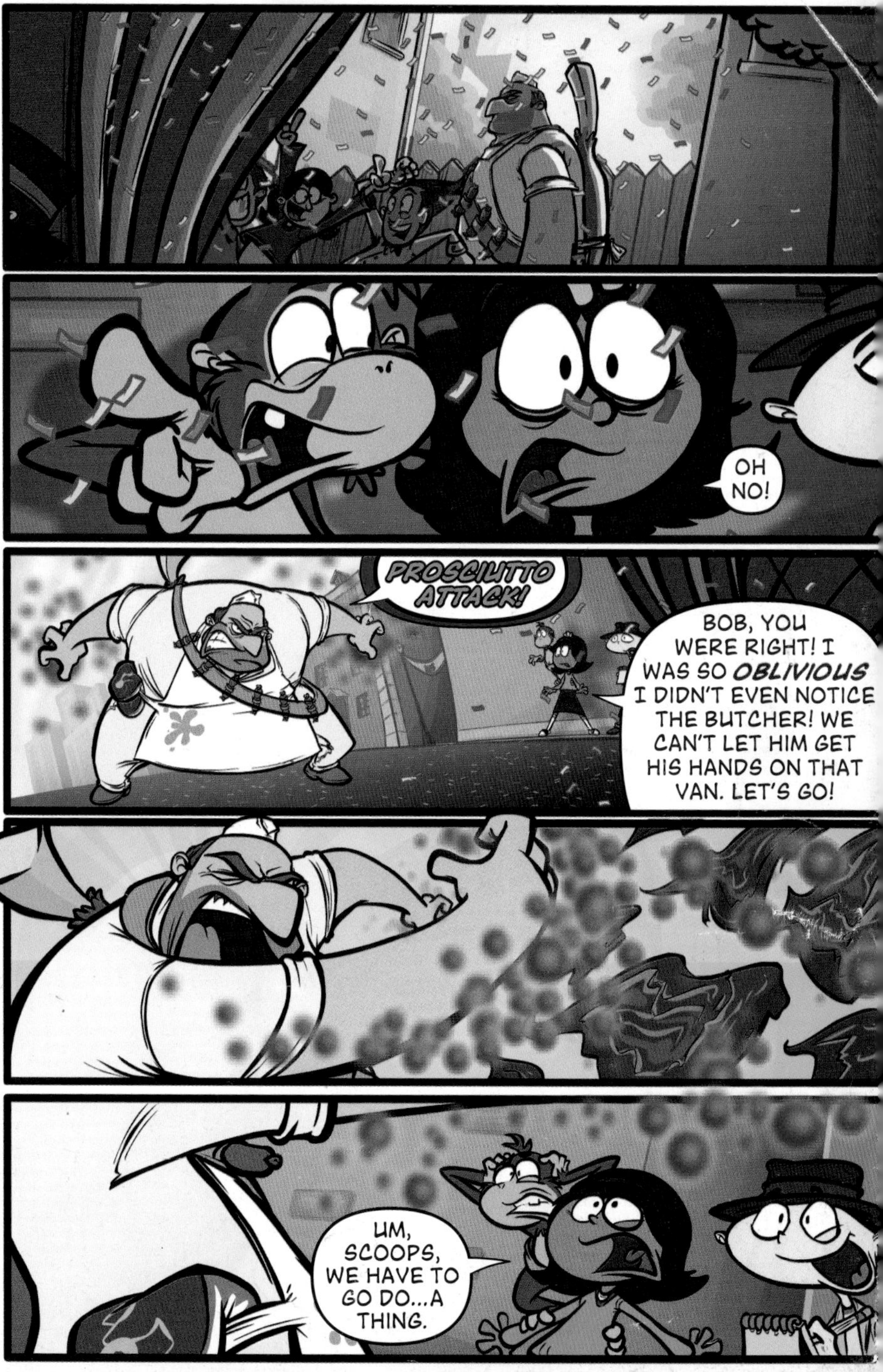
OH NO!
PROSCIUTTO ATTACK!
BOB, YOU WERE RIGHT! I WAS SO *OBLIVIOUS* I DIDN'T EVEN NOTICE THE BUTCHER! WE CAN'T LET HIM GET HIS HANDS ON THAT VAN. LET'S GO!
UM, SCOOPS, WE HAVE TO GO DO...A THING.

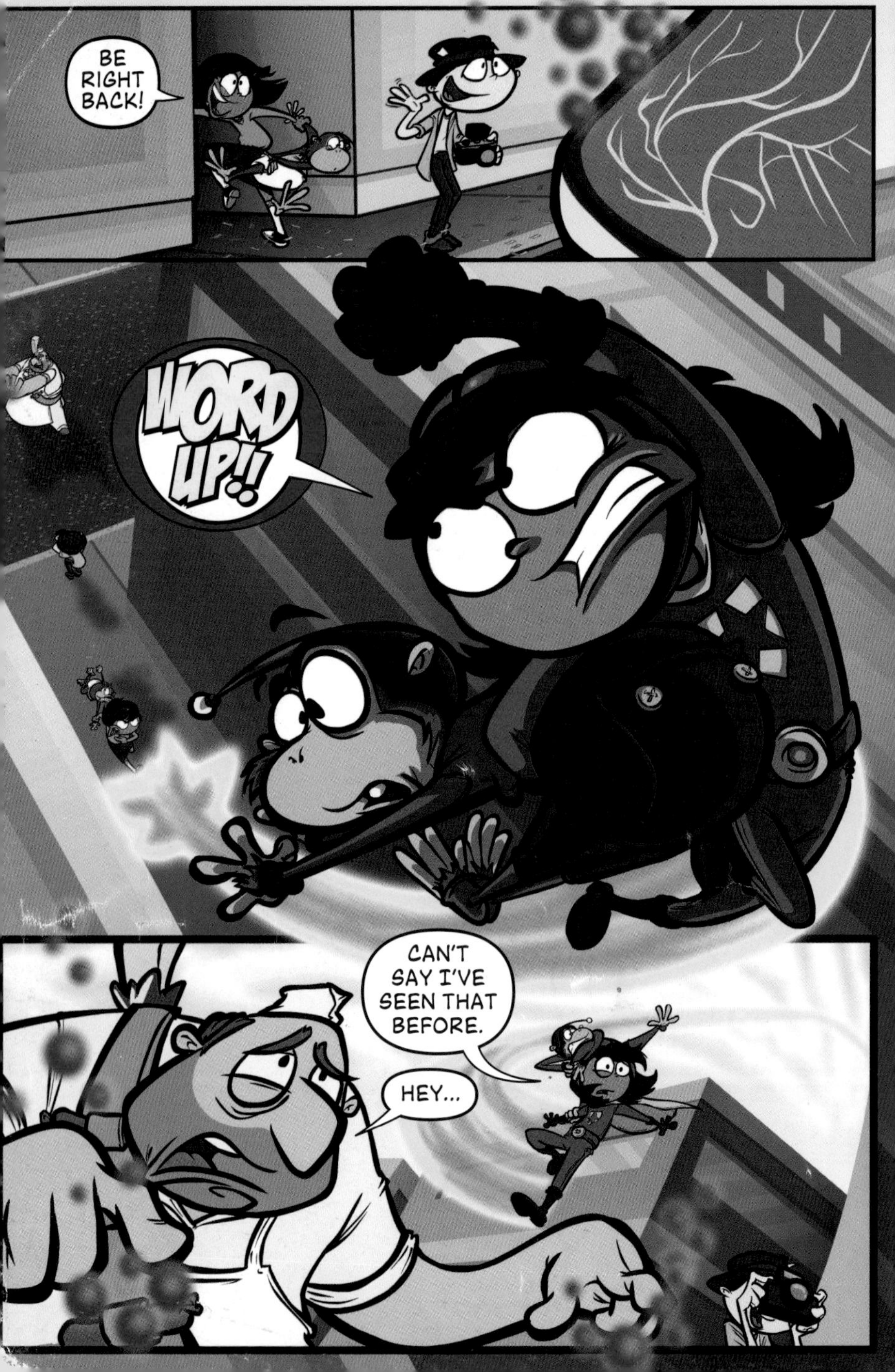
BE RIGHT BACK!
WORD UP!!
CAN'T SAY I'VE SEEN THAT BEFORE.
HEY...

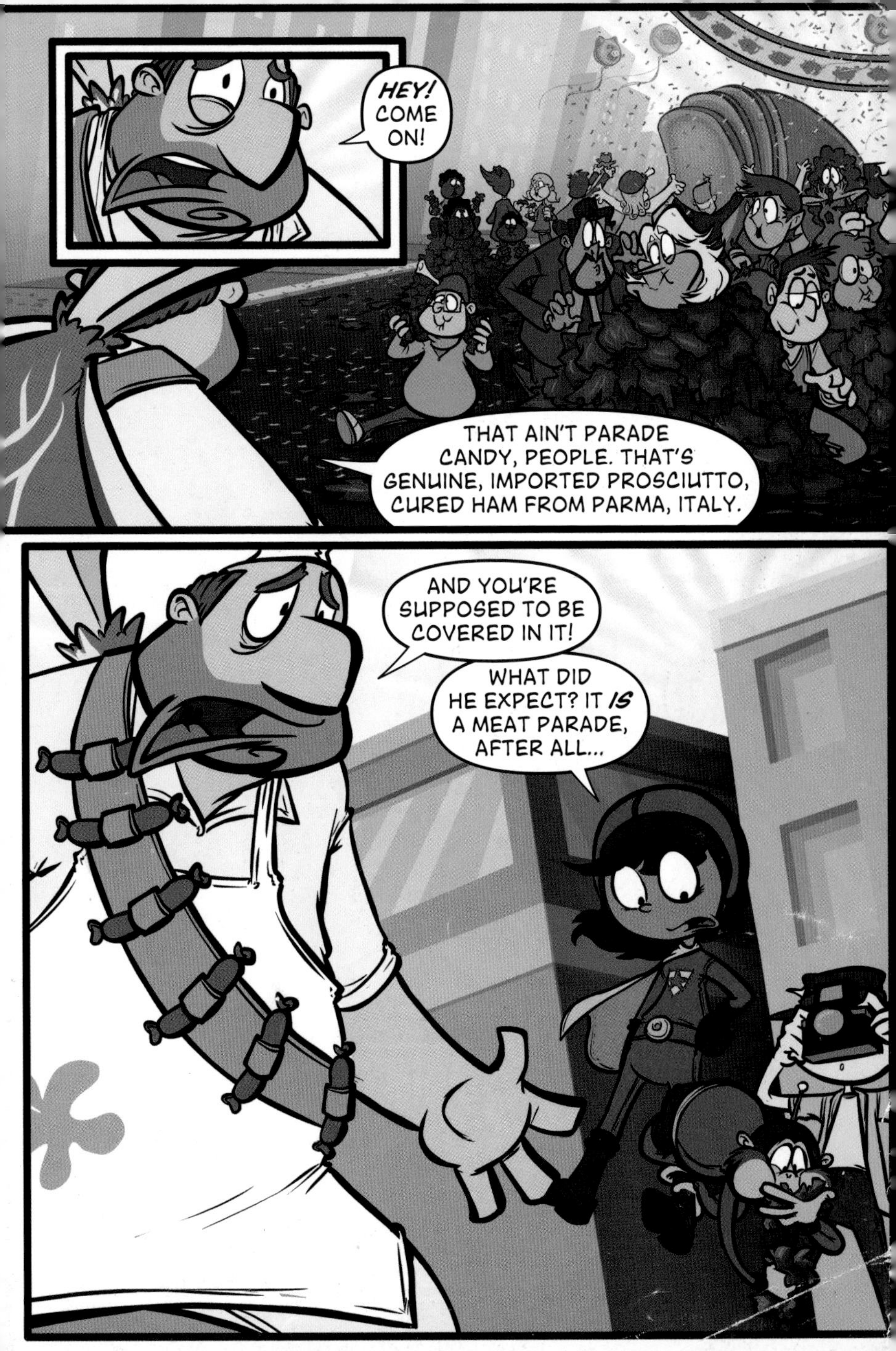
HEY! COME ON!
THAT AIN'T PARADE CANDY, PEOPLE. THAT'S GENUINE, IMPORTED PROSCIUTTO, CURED HAM FROM PARMA, ITALY.
AND YOU'RE SUPPOSED TO BE COVERED IN IT!
WHAT DID HE EXPECT? IT *IS* A MEAT PARADE, AFTER ALL...

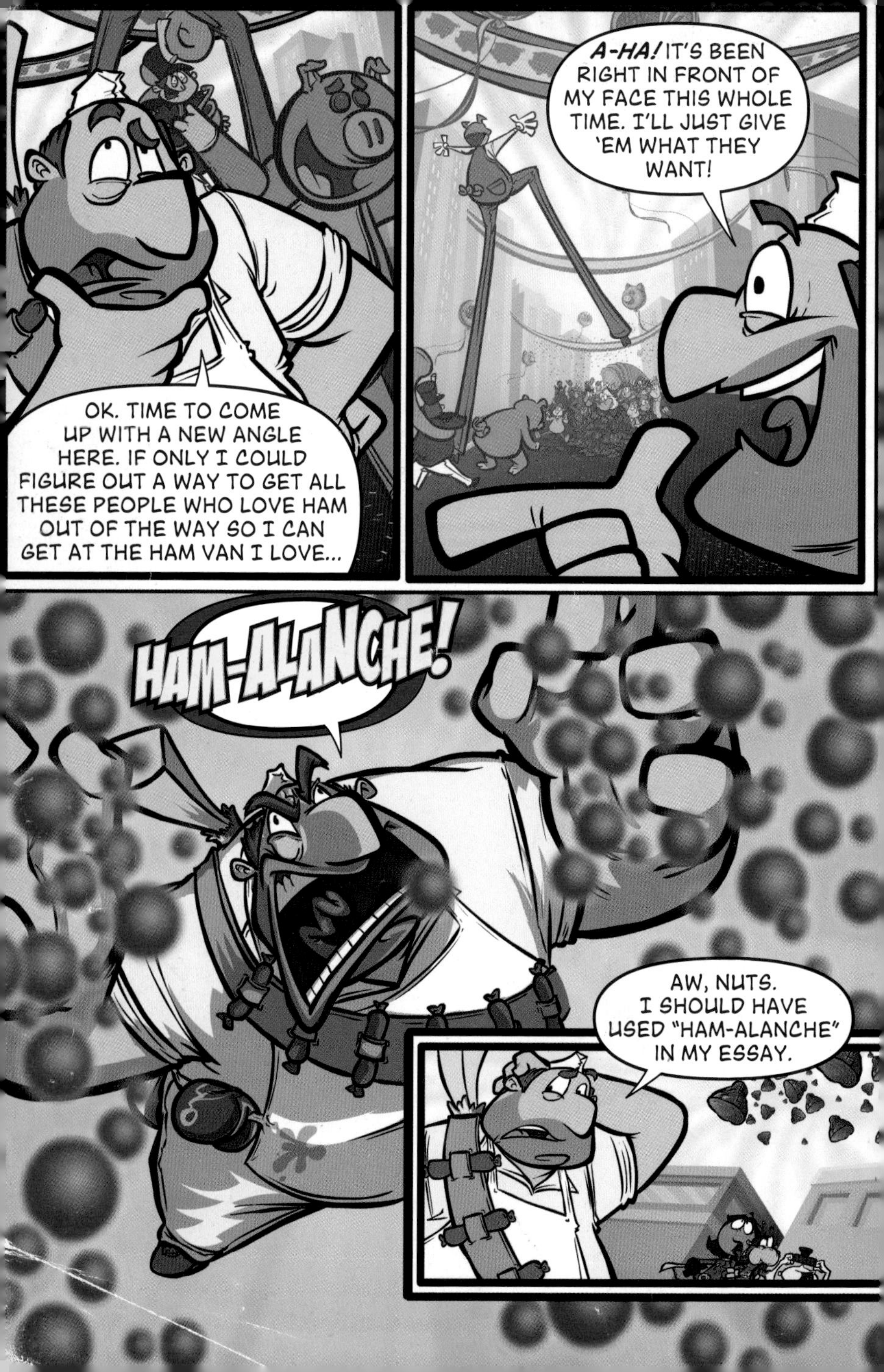
OK. TIME TO COME UP WITH A NEW ANGLE HERE. IF ONLY I COULD FIGURE OUT A WAY TO GET ALL THESE PEOPLE WHO LOVE HAM OUT OF THE WAY SO I CAN GET AT THE HAM VAN I LOVE...
A-HA! IT'S BEEN RIGHT IN FRONT OF MY FACE THIS WHOLE TIME. I'LL JUST GIVE 'EM WHAT THEY WANT!
HAM-ALANCHE!
AW, NUTS. I SHOULD HAVE USED "HAM-ALANCHE" IN MY ESSAY.

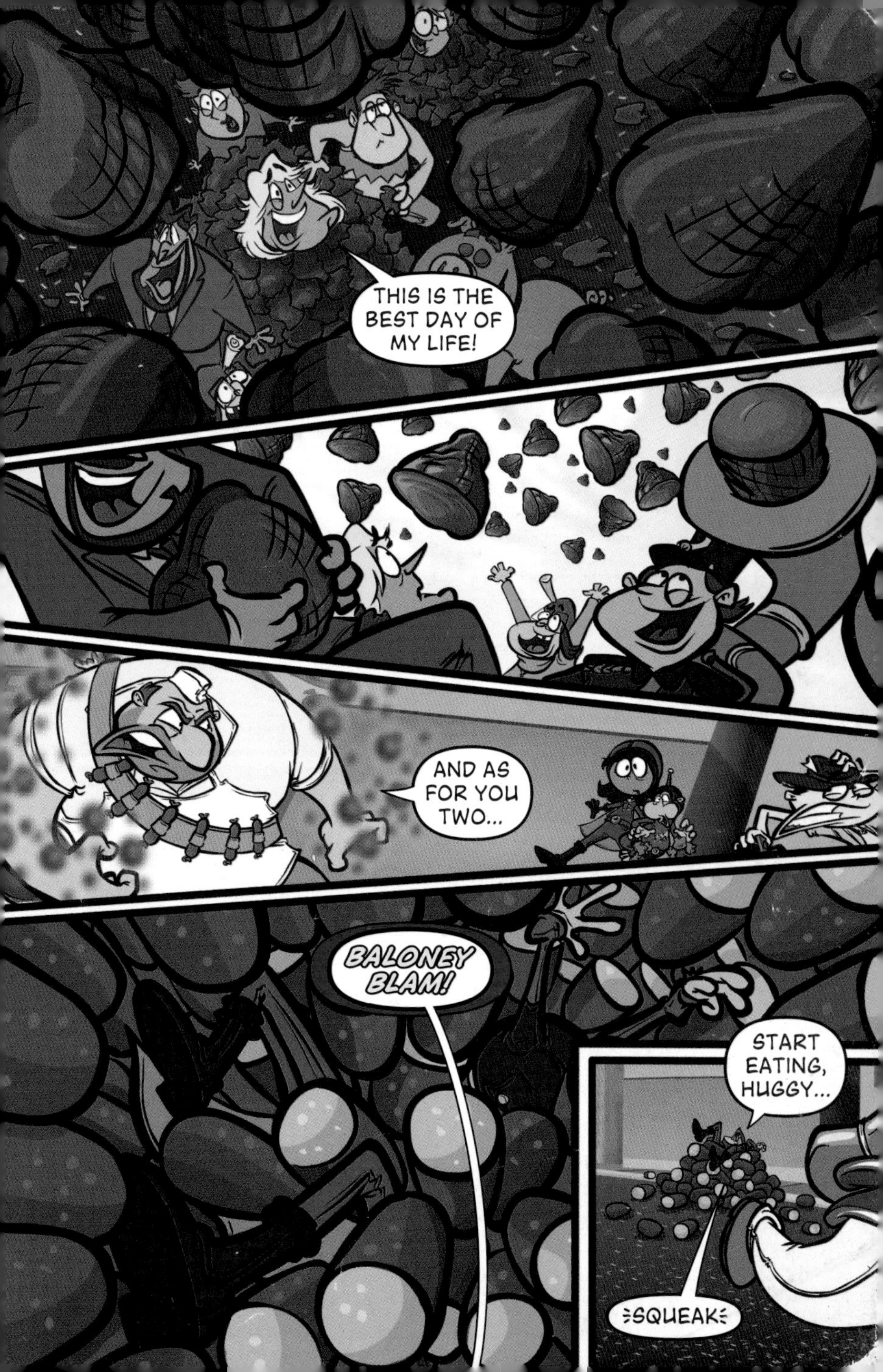
THIS IS THE BEST DAY OF MY LIFE!
AND AS FOR YOU TWO...
BALONEY BLAM!
START EATING, HUGGY...
SQUEAK

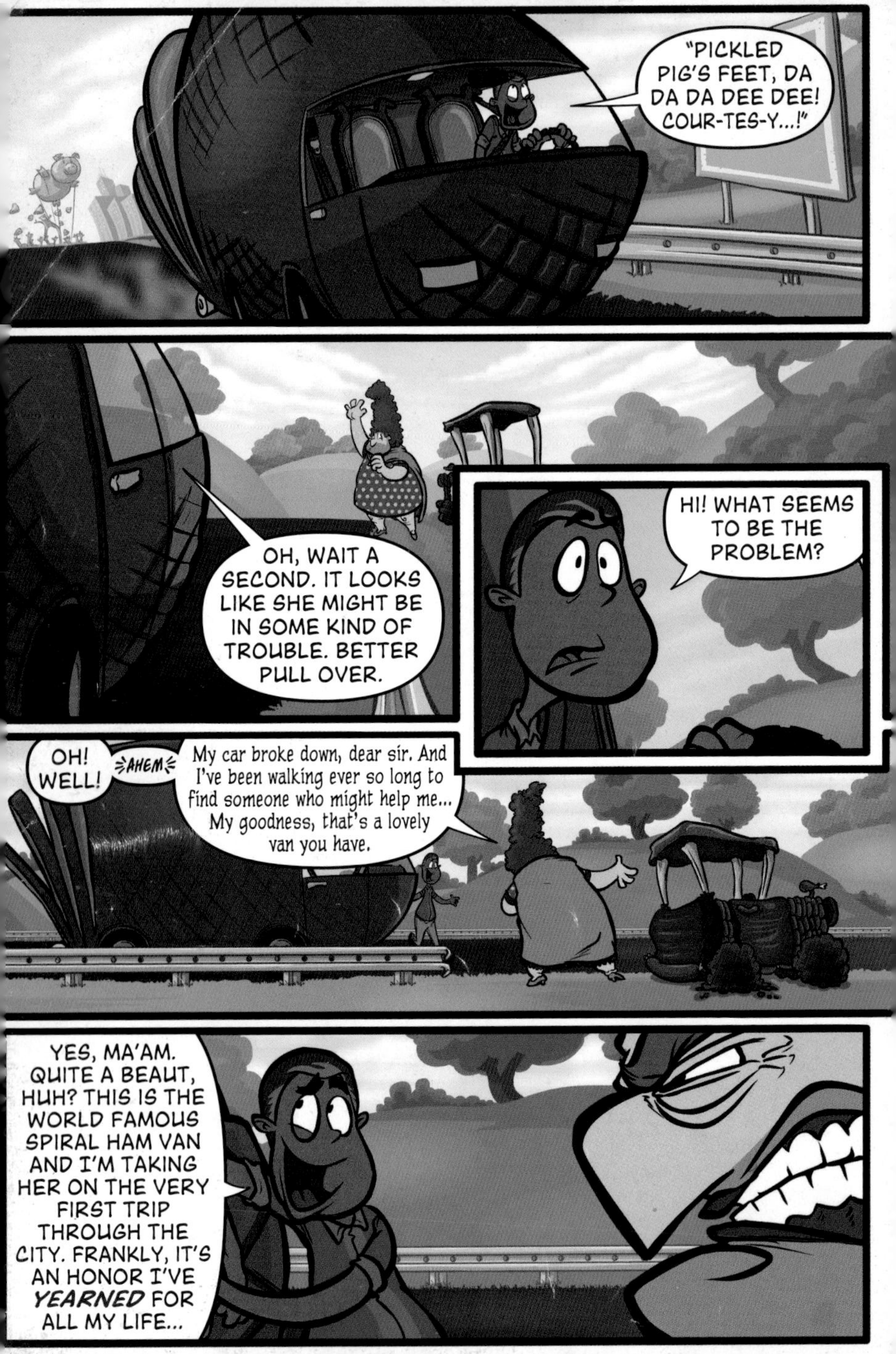
"PICKLED PIG'S FEET, DA DA DA DEE DEE! COUR-TES-Y...!"
OH, WAIT A SECOND. IT LOOKS LIKE SHE MIGHT BE IN SOME KIND OF TROUBLE. BETTER PULL OVER.
HI! WHAT SEEMS TO BE THE PROBLEM?
OH! WELL!
AHEM
My car broke down, dear sir. And I've been walking ever so long to find someone who might help me... My goodness, that's a lovely van you have.
YES, MA'AM. QUITE A BEAUT, HUH? THIS IS THE WORLD FAMOUS SPIRAL HAM VAN AND I'M TAKING HER ON THE VERY FIRST TRIP THROUGH THE CITY. FRANKLY, IT'S AN HONOR I'VE *YEARNED* FOR ALL MY LIFE...

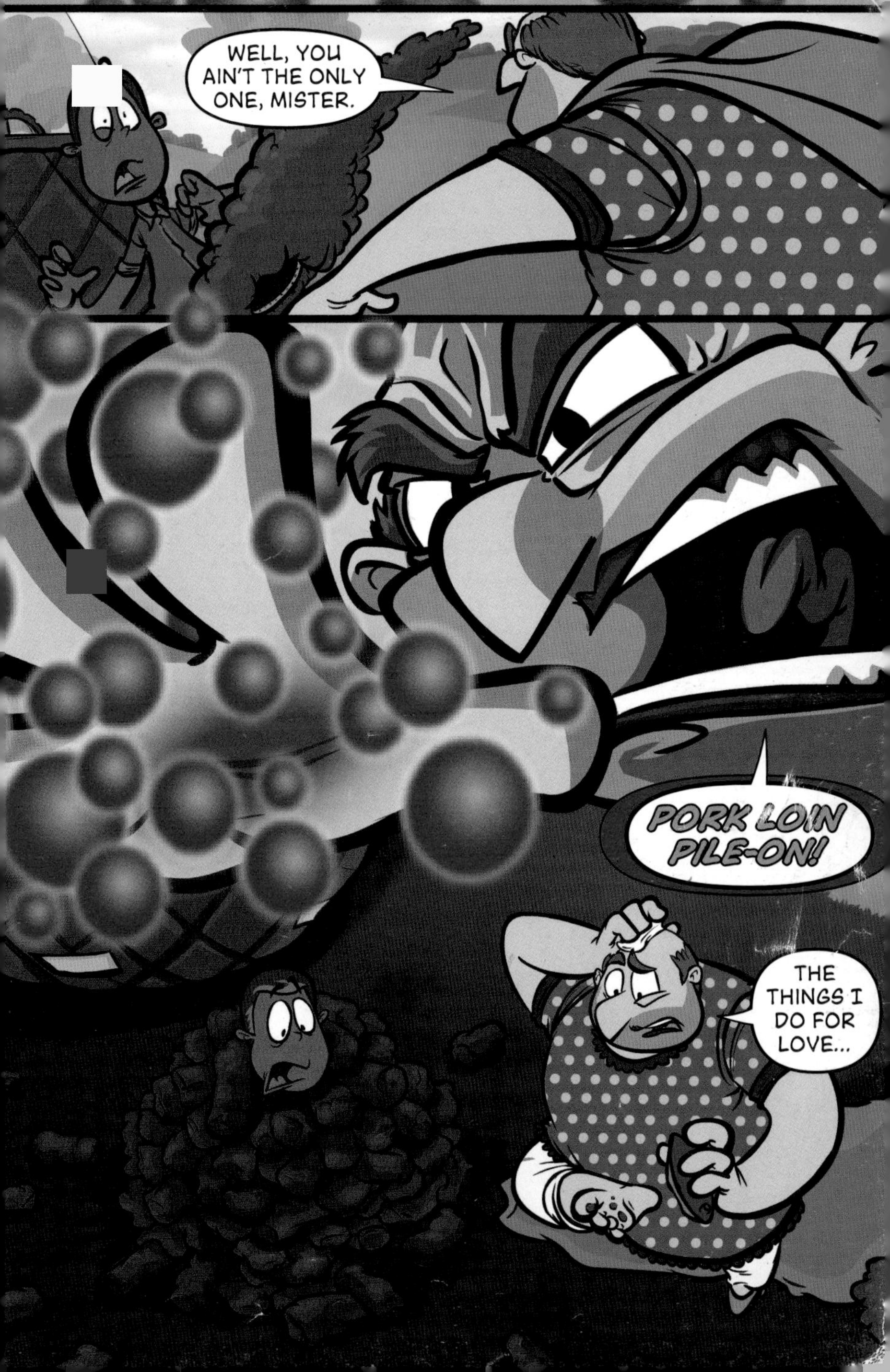
WELL, YOU AIN'T THE ONLY ONE, MISTER.
PORK LOIN PILE-ON!
THE THINGS I DO FOR LOVE...

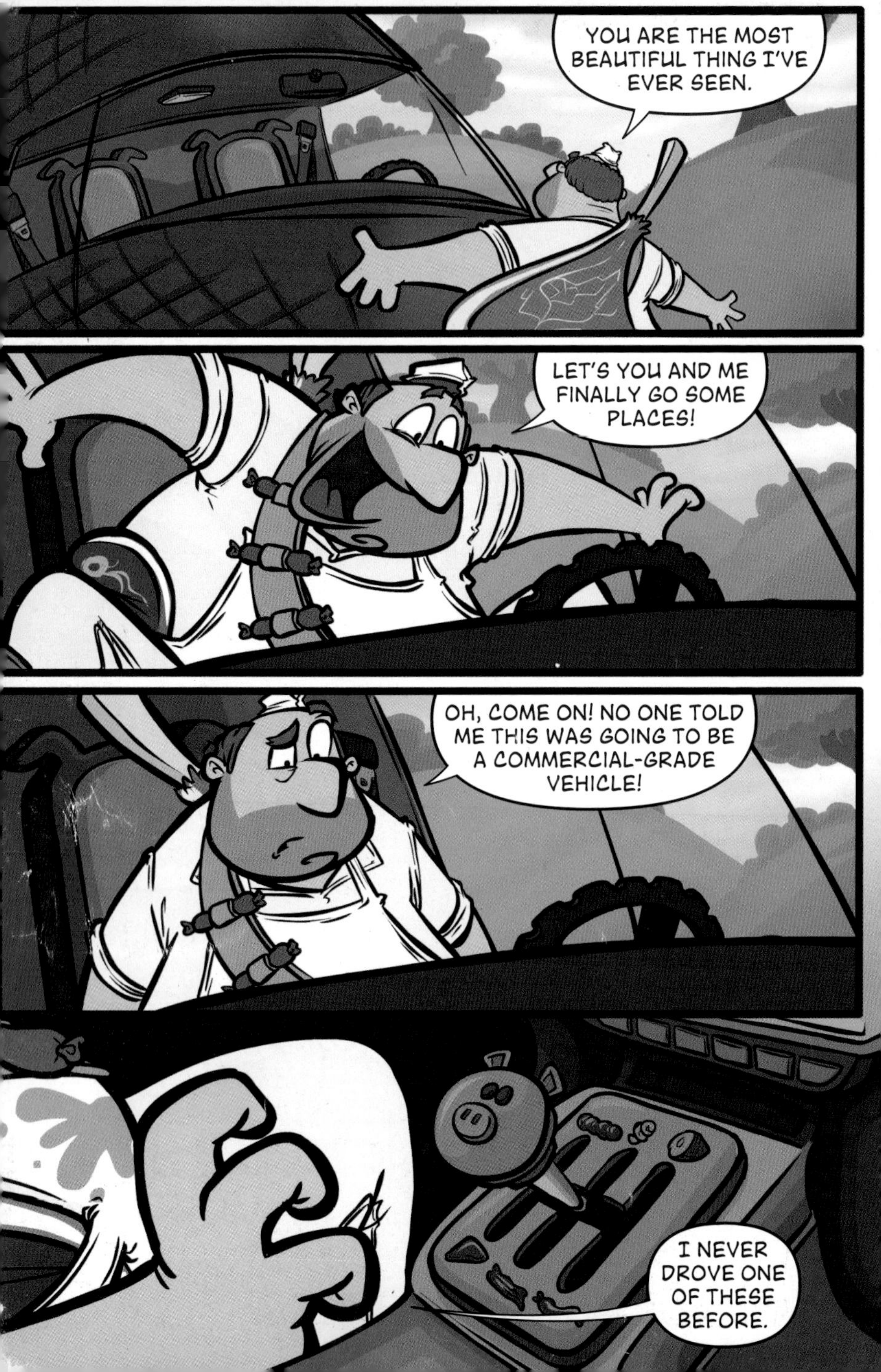
YOU ARE THE MOST BEAUTIFUL THING I'VE EVER SEEN.
LET'S YOU AND ME FINALLY GO SOME PLACES!
OH, COME ON! NO ONE TOLD ME THIS WAS GOING TO BE A COMMERCIAL-GRADE VEHICLE!
I NEVER DROVE ONE OF THESE BEFORE.

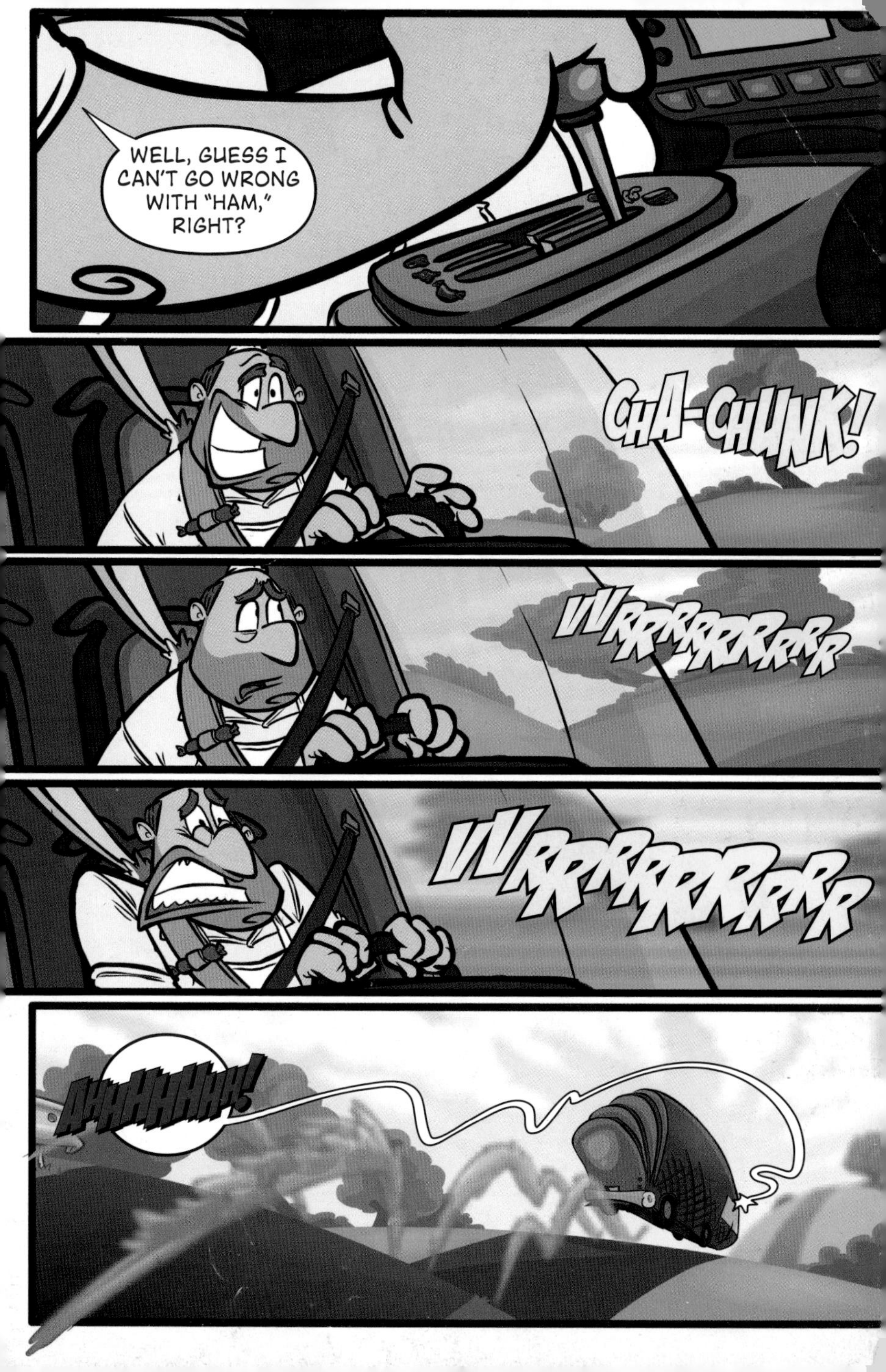
WELL, GUESS I CAN'T GO WRONG WITH "HAM," RIGHT?
CHA-CHUNK!
VVRRRRRRRRR
VVRRRRRRRRRR
AHHHHHHH!

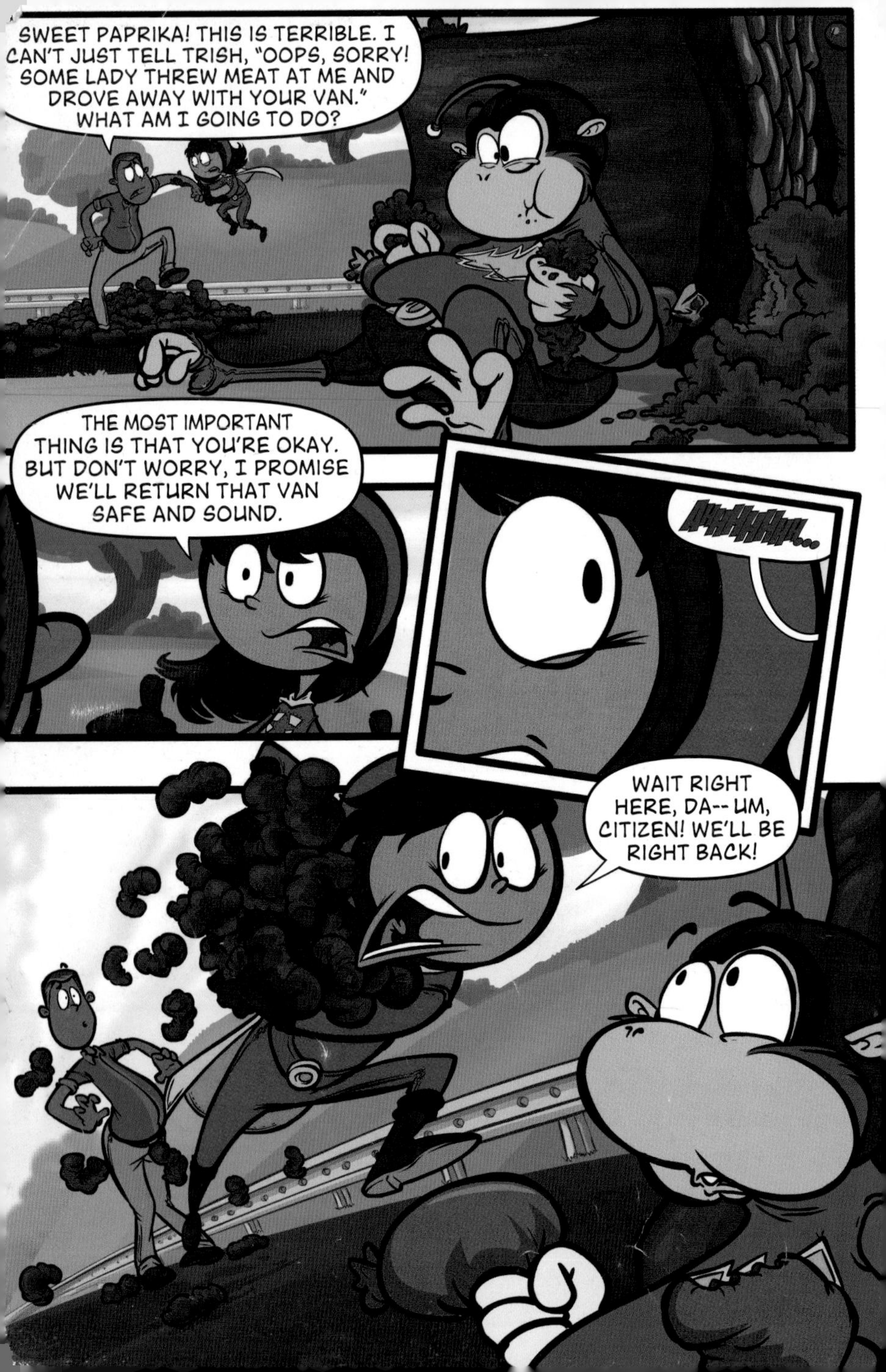
SWEET PAPRIKA! THIS IS TERRIBLE. I CAN'T JUST TELL TRISH, "OOPS, SORRY! SOME LADY THREW MEAT AT ME AND DROVE AWAY WITH YOUR VAN." WHAT AM I GOING TO DO?
THE MOST IMPORTANT THING IS THAT YOU'RE OKAY. BUT DON'T WORRY, I PROMISE WE'LL RETURN THAT VAN SAFE AND SOUND.
WAIT RIGHT HERE, DA-- UM, CITIZEN! WE'LL BE RIGHT BACK!

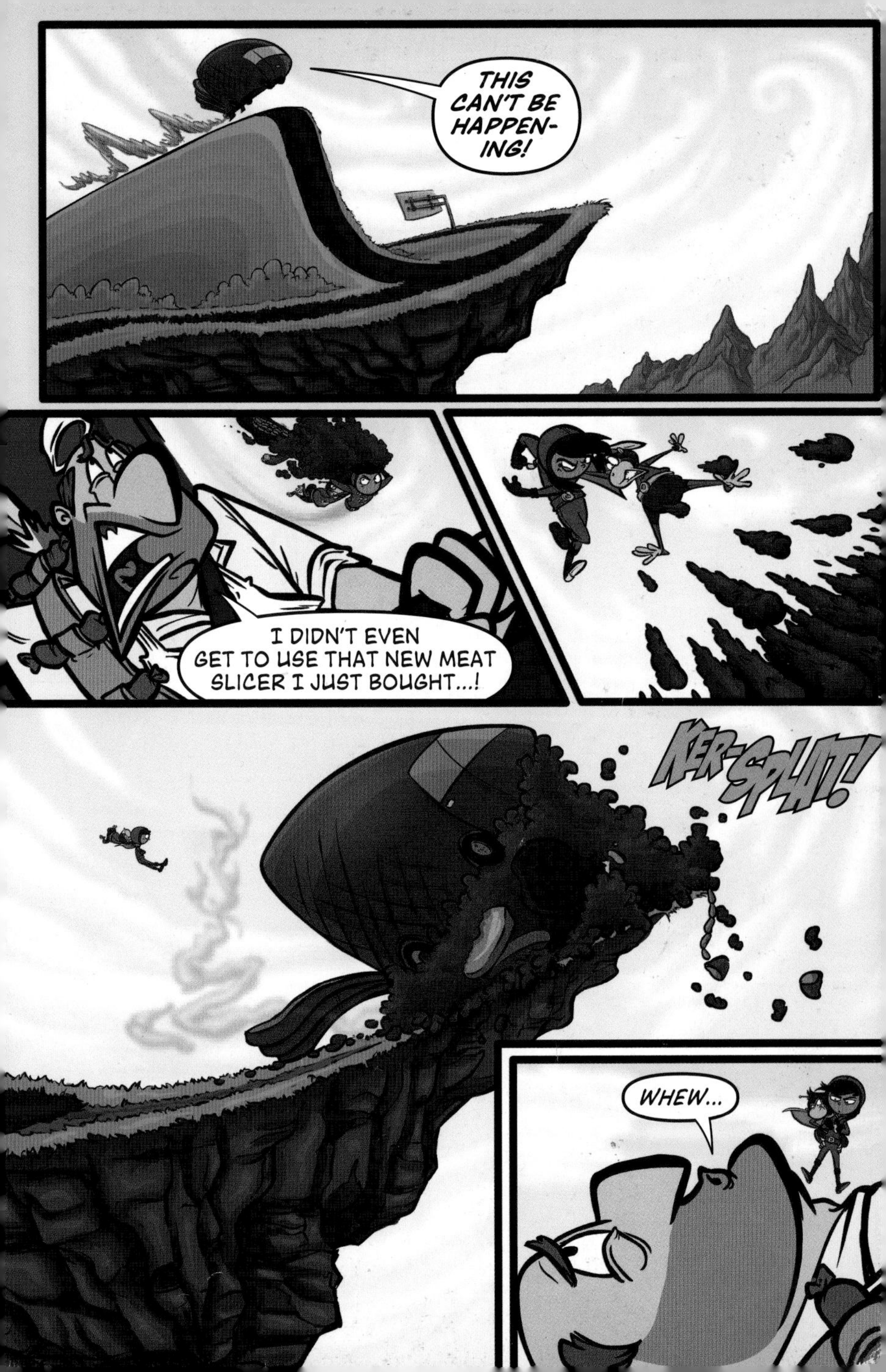
THIS CAN'T BE HAPPENING!
I DIDN'T EVEN GET TO USE THAT NEW MEAT SLICER I JUST BOUGHT...!
KER-SPLATT!
WHEW...

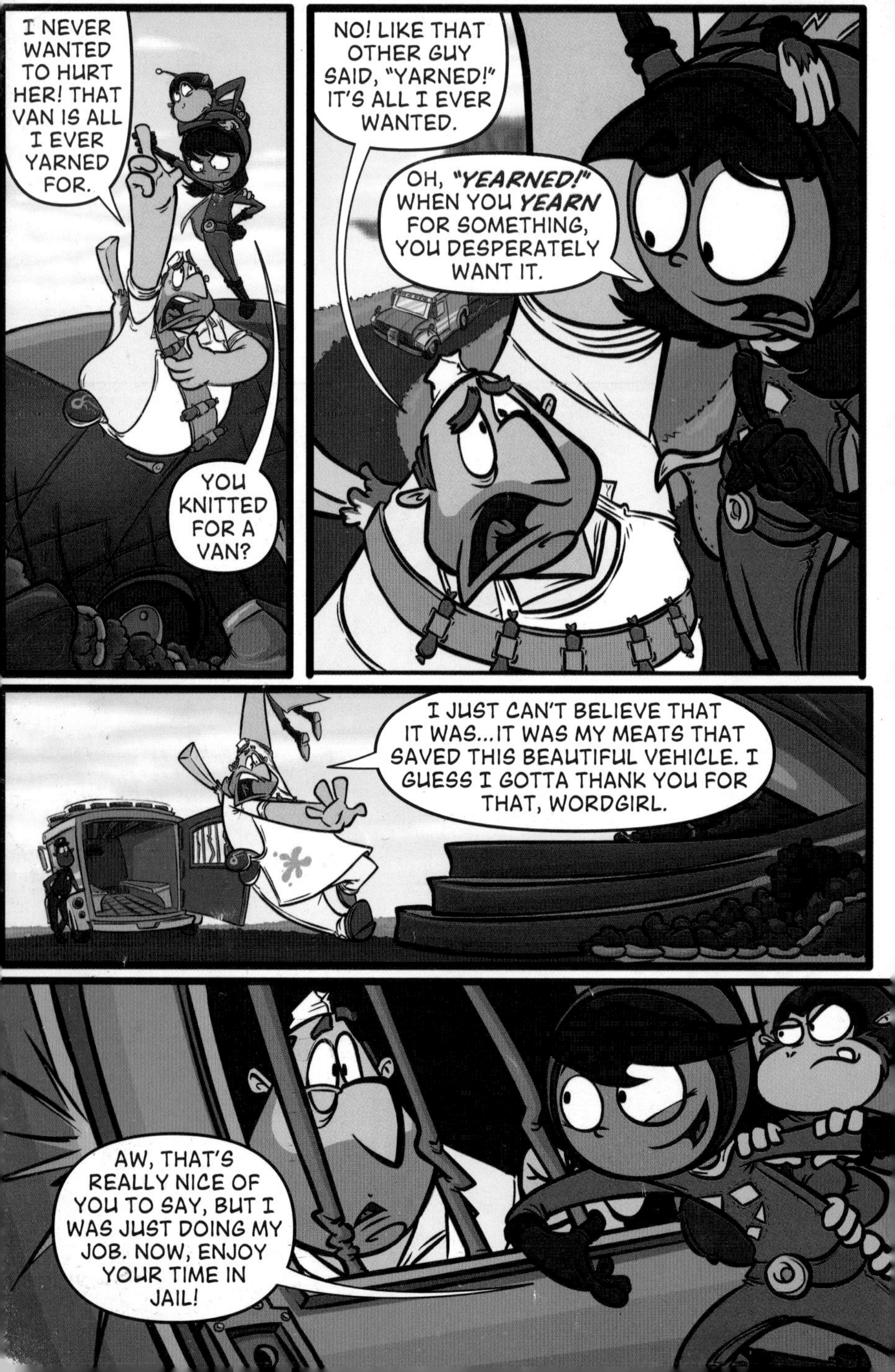
I NEVER WANTED TO HURT HER! THAT VAN IS ALL I EVER YARNED FOR.
YOU KNITTED FOR A VAN?
NO! LIKE THAT OTHER GUY SAID, "YARNED!" IT'S ALL I EVER WANTED.
OH, "YEARNED!" WHEN YOU YEARN FOR SOMETHING, YOU DESPERATELY WANT IT.
I JUST CAN'T BELIEVE THAT IT WAS...IT WAS MY MEATS THAT SAVED THIS BEAUTIFUL VEHICLE. I GUESS I GOTTA THANK YOU FOR THAT, WORDGIRL.
AW, THAT'S REALLY NICE OF YOU TO SAY, BUT I WAS JUST DOING MY JOB. NOW, ENJOY YOUR TIME IN JAIL!

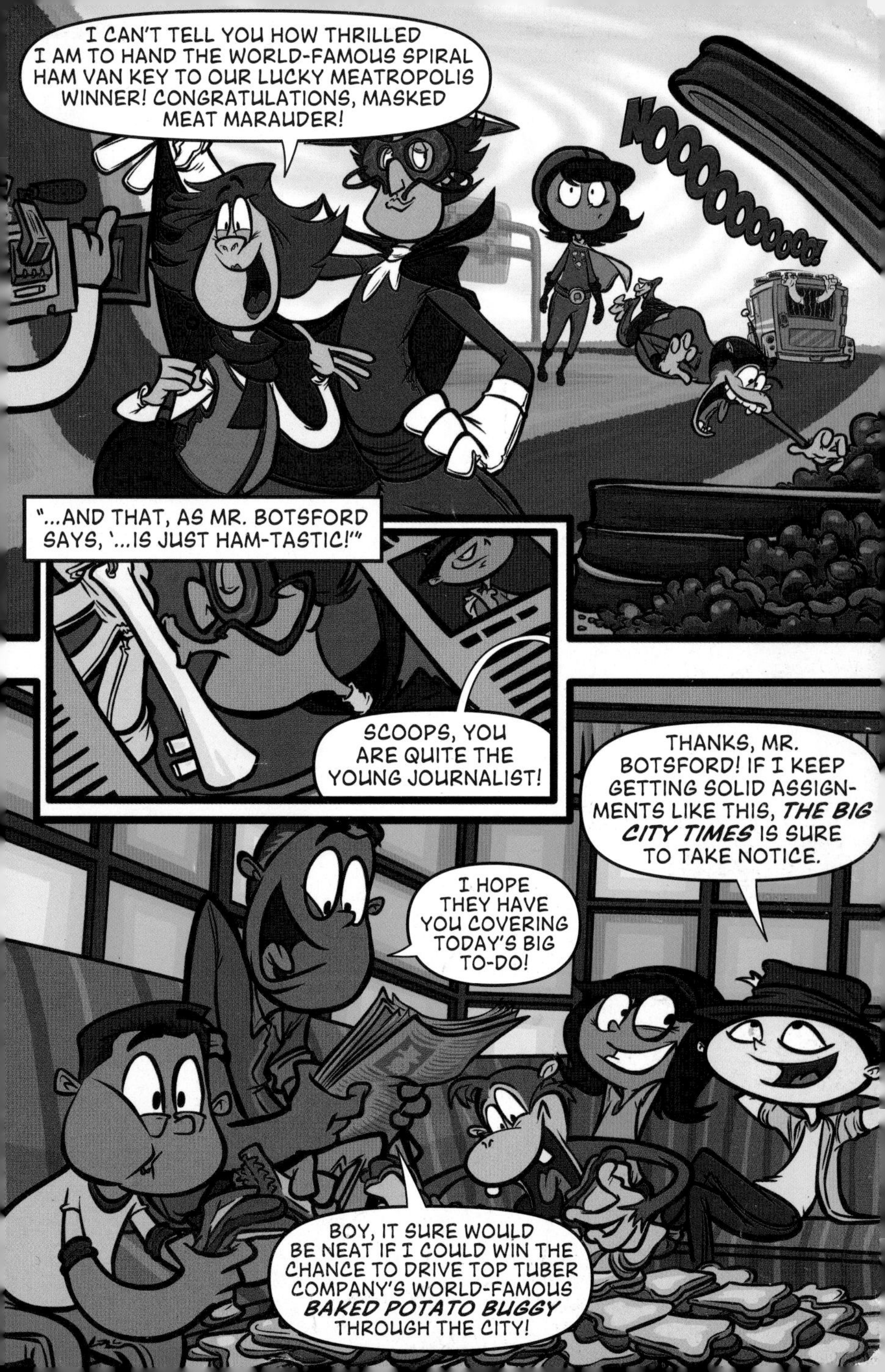
I CAN'T TELL YOU HOW THRILLED I AM TO HAND THE WORLD-FAMOUS SPIRAL HAM VAN KEY TO OUR LUCKY MEATROPOLIS WINNER! CONGRATULATIONS, MASKED MEAT MARAUDER!
NOOOOOOOOOOOOO!
"...AND THAT, AS MR. BOTSFORD SAYS, '...IS JUST HAM-TASTIC!'"
SCOOPS, YOU ARE QUITE THE YOUNG JOURNALIST!
THANKS, MR. BOTSFORD! IF I KEEP GETTING SOLID ASSIGNMENTS LIKE THIS, *THE BIG CITY TIMES* IS SURE TO TAKE NOTICE.
I HOPE THEY HAVE YOU COVERING TODAY'S BIG TO-DO!
BOY, IT SURE WOULD BE NEAT IF I COULD WIN THE CHANCE TO DRIVE TOP TUBER COMPANY'S WORLD-FAMOUS ***BAKED POTATO BUGGY*** THROUGH THE CITY!

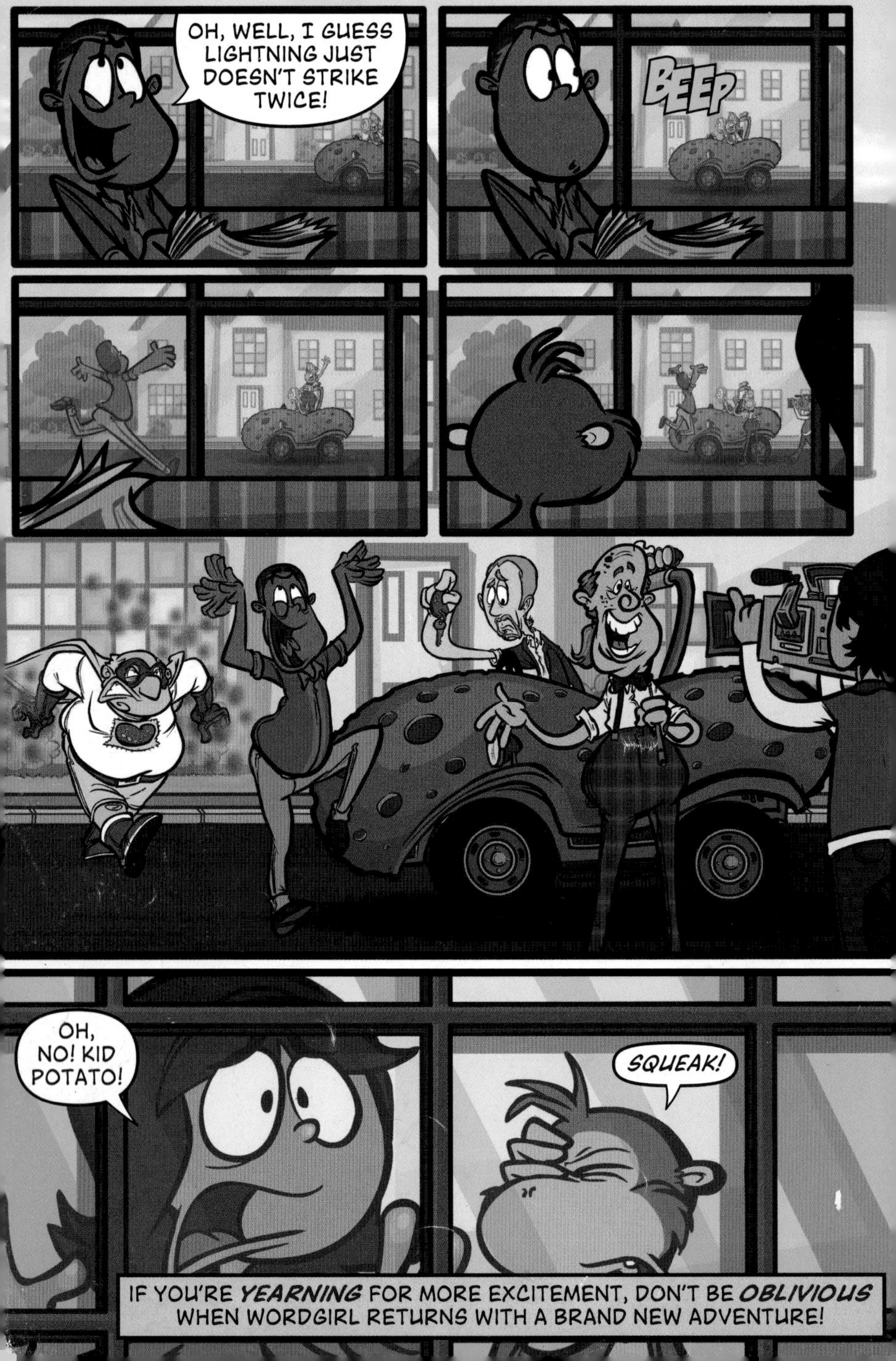
OH, WELL, I GUESS LIGHTNING JUST DOESN'T STRIKE TWICE!
BEEP
OH, NO! KID POTATO!
SQUEAK!
IF YOU'RE *YEARNING* FOR MORE EXCITEMENT, DON'T BE *OBLIVIOUS* WHEN WORDGIRL RETURNS WITH A BRAND NEW ADVENTURE!

THINK BIG

Scott Ganz & Andrew Samson
WRITERS

Andy Price
ART

Lisa Moore
COLORS

Steve Wands
LETTERS

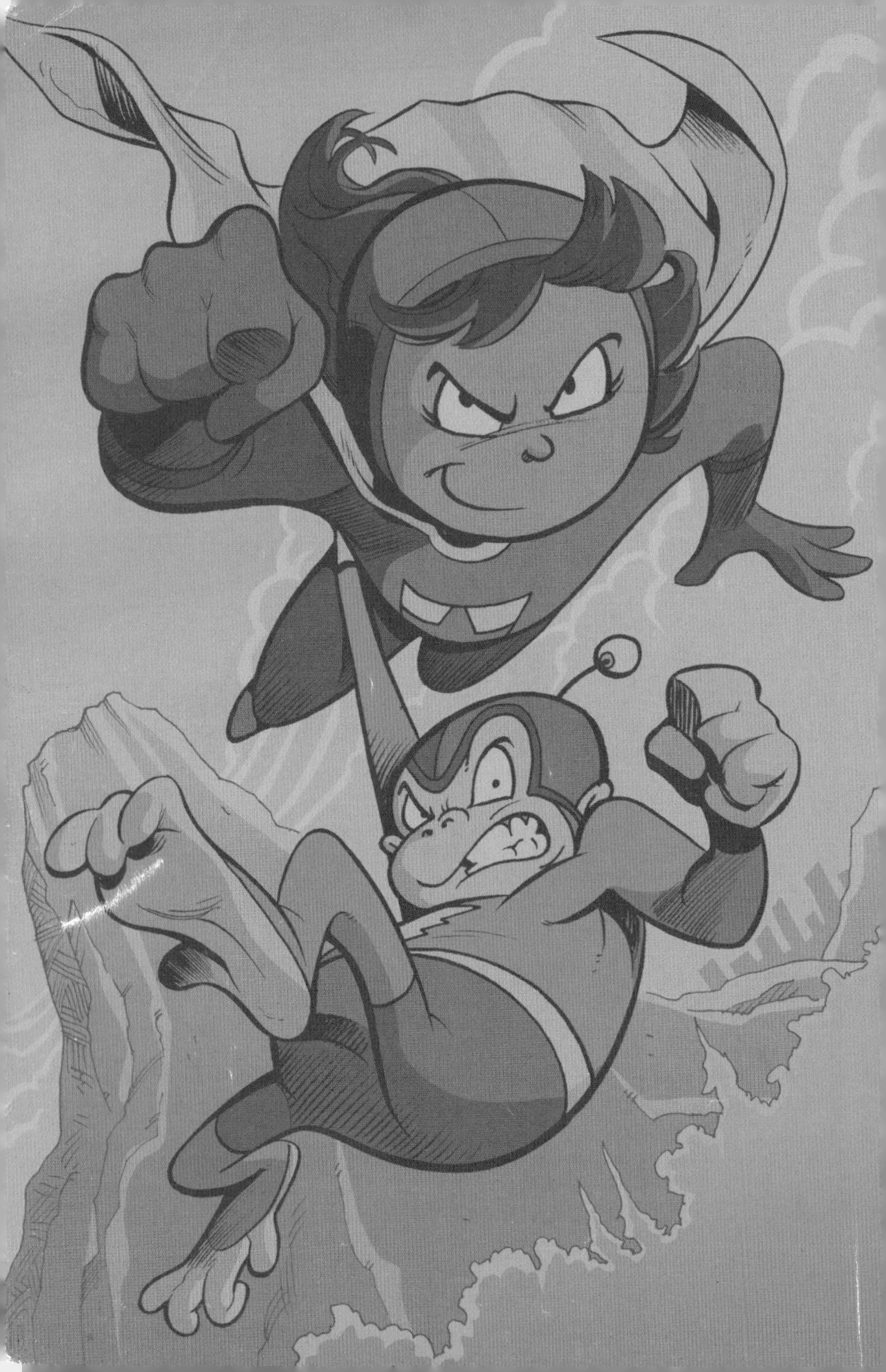

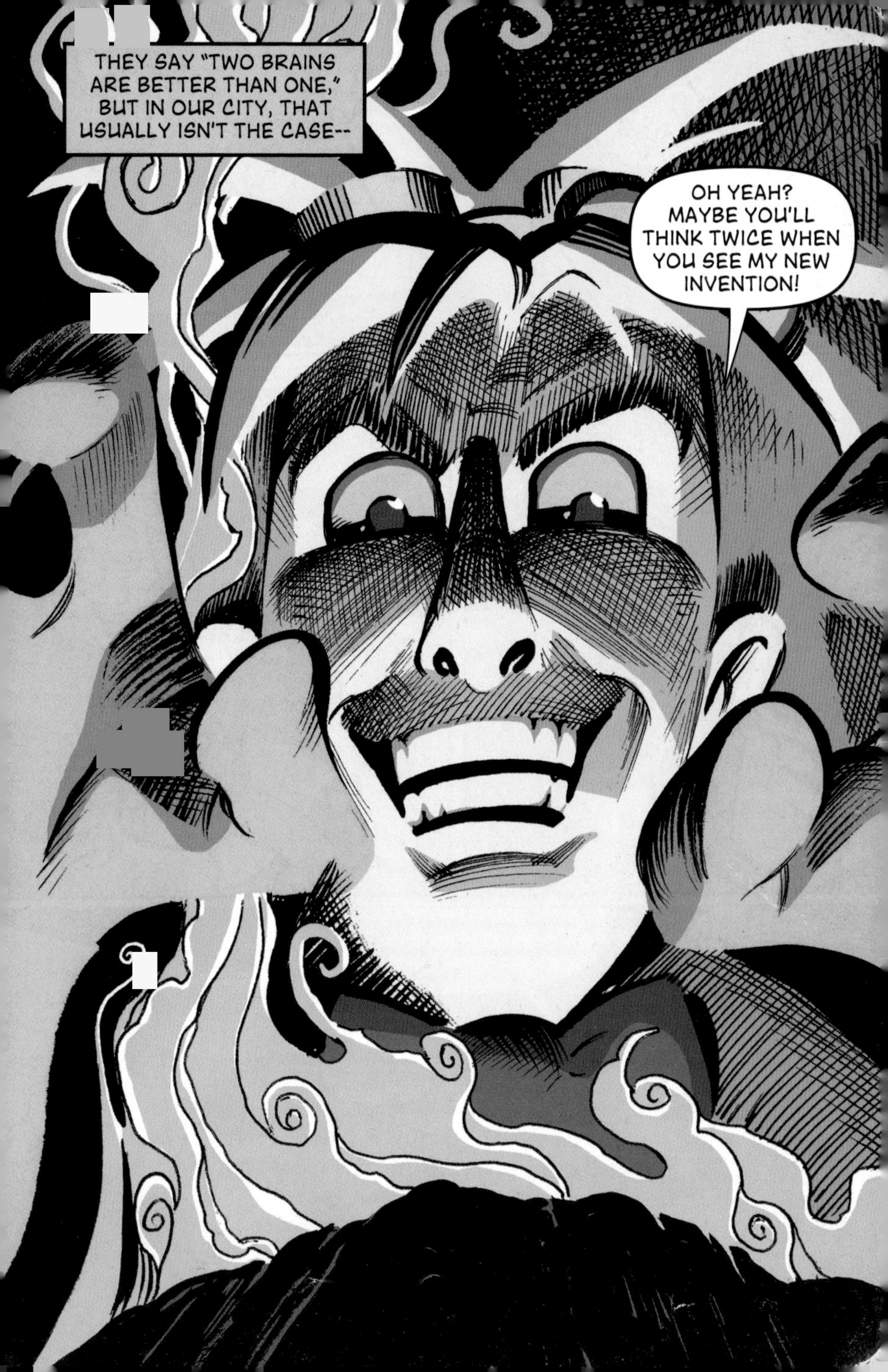
THEY SAY "TWO BRAINS ARE BETTER THAN ONE," BUT IN OUR CITY, THAT USUALLY ISN'T THE CASE--
OH YEAH? MAYBE YOU'LL THINK TWICE WHEN YOU SEE MY NEW INVENTION!

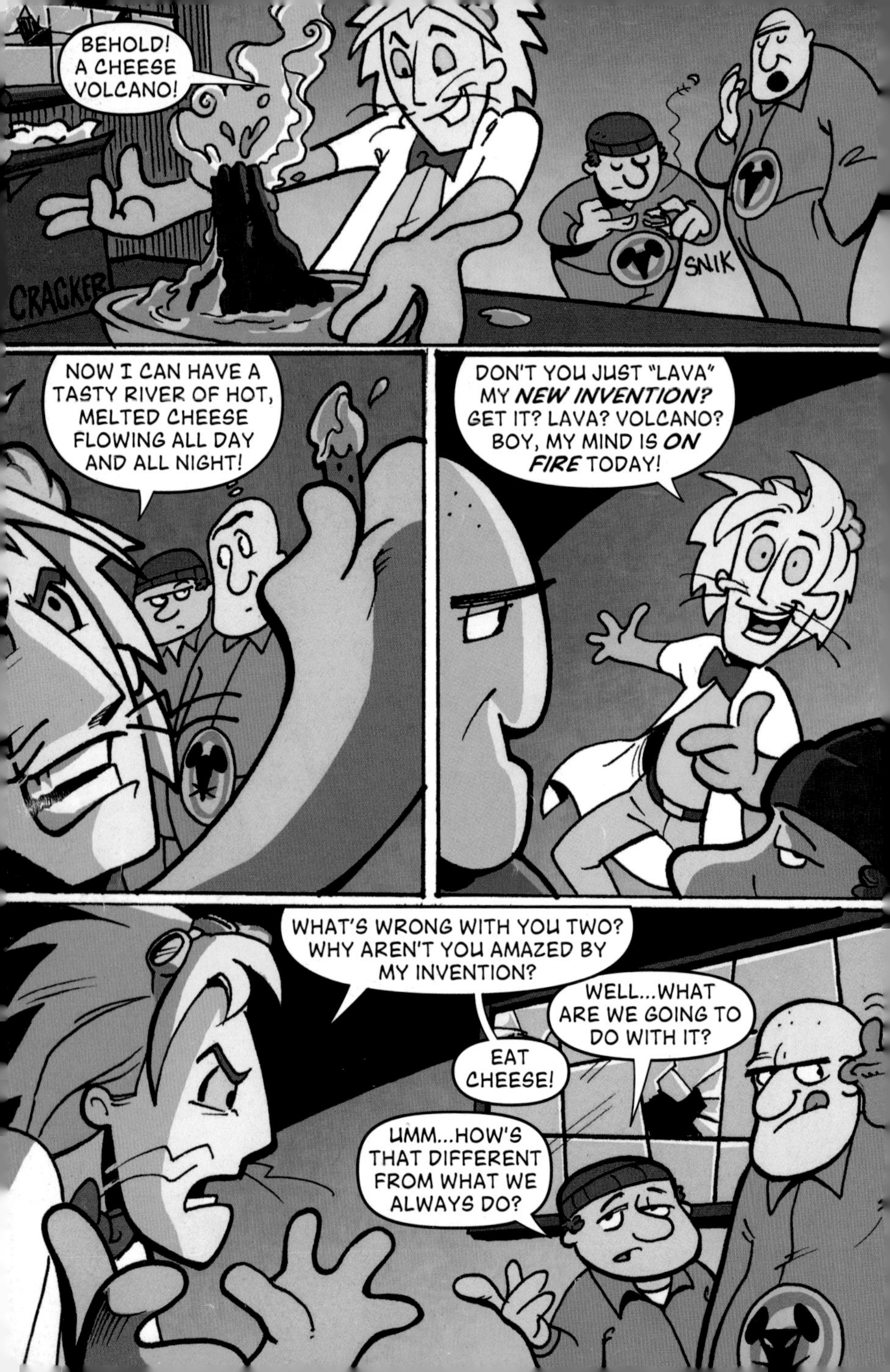

BEHOLD! A CHEESE VOLCANO!
CRACKER
SNIK
NOW I CAN HAVE A TASTY RIVER OF HOT, MELTED CHEESE FLOWING ALL DAY AND ALL NIGHT!
DON'T YOU JUST "LAVA" MY NEW INVENTION? GET IT? LAVA? VOLCANO? BOY, MY MIND IS ON FIRE TODAY!
WHAT'S WRONG WITH YOU TWO? WHY AREN'T YOU AMAZED BY MY INVENTION?
WELL...WHAT ARE WE GOING TO DO WITH IT?
EAT CHEESE!
UMM...HOW'S THAT DIFFERENT FROM WHAT WE ALWAYS DO?

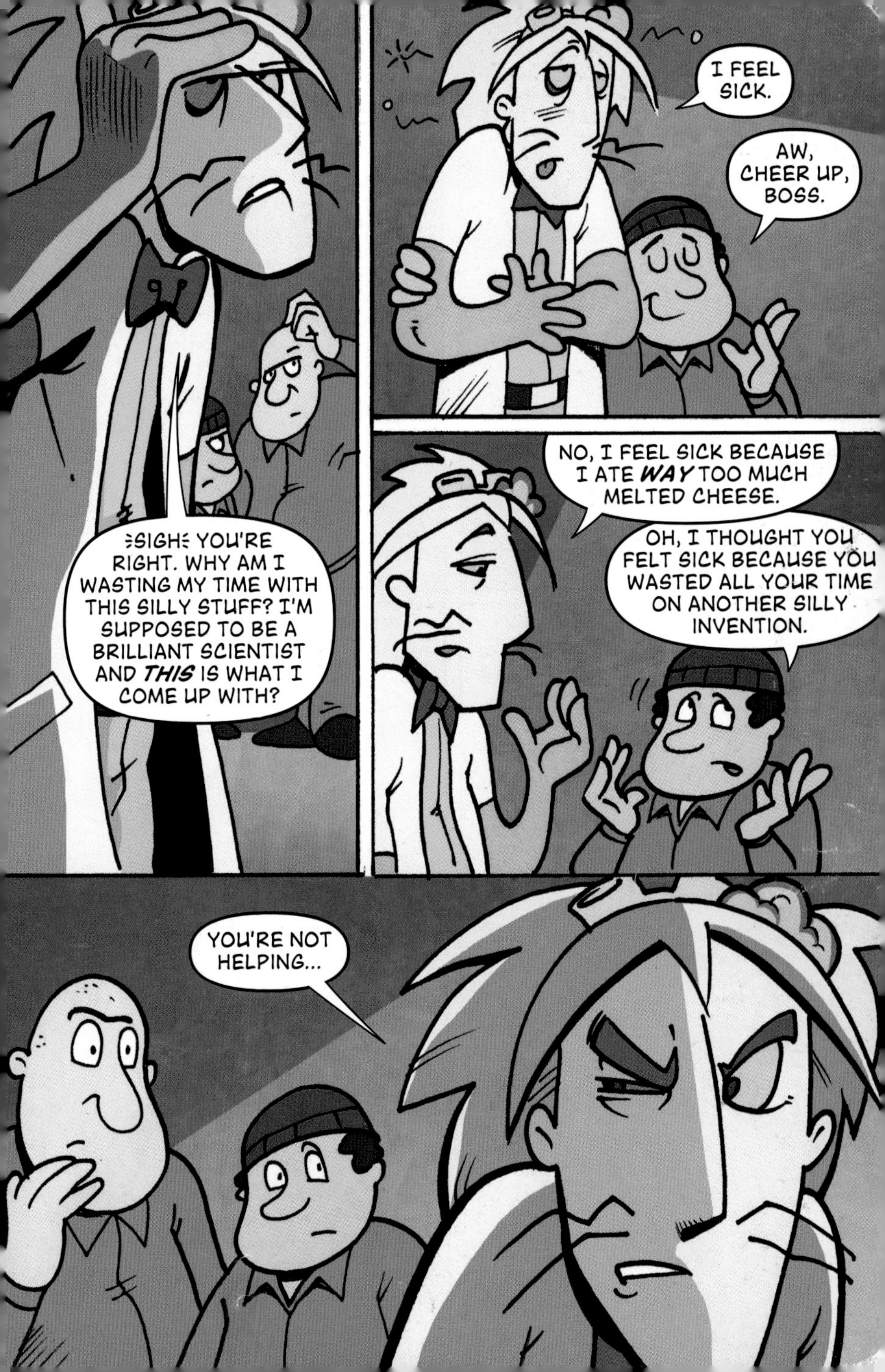

⁝SIGH⁝ YOU'RE RIGHT. WHY AM I WASTING MY TIME WITH THIS SILLY STUFF? I'M SUPPOSED TO BE A BRILLIANT SCIENTIST AND *THIS* IS WHAT I COME UP WITH?
I FEEL SICK.
AW, CHEER UP, BOSS.
NO, I FEEL SICK BECAUSE I ATE ***WAY*** TOO MUCH MELTED CHEESE.
OH, I THOUGHT YOU FELT SICK BECAUSE YOU WASTED ALL YOUR TIME ON ANOTHER SILLY INVENTION.
YOU'RE NOT HELPING...

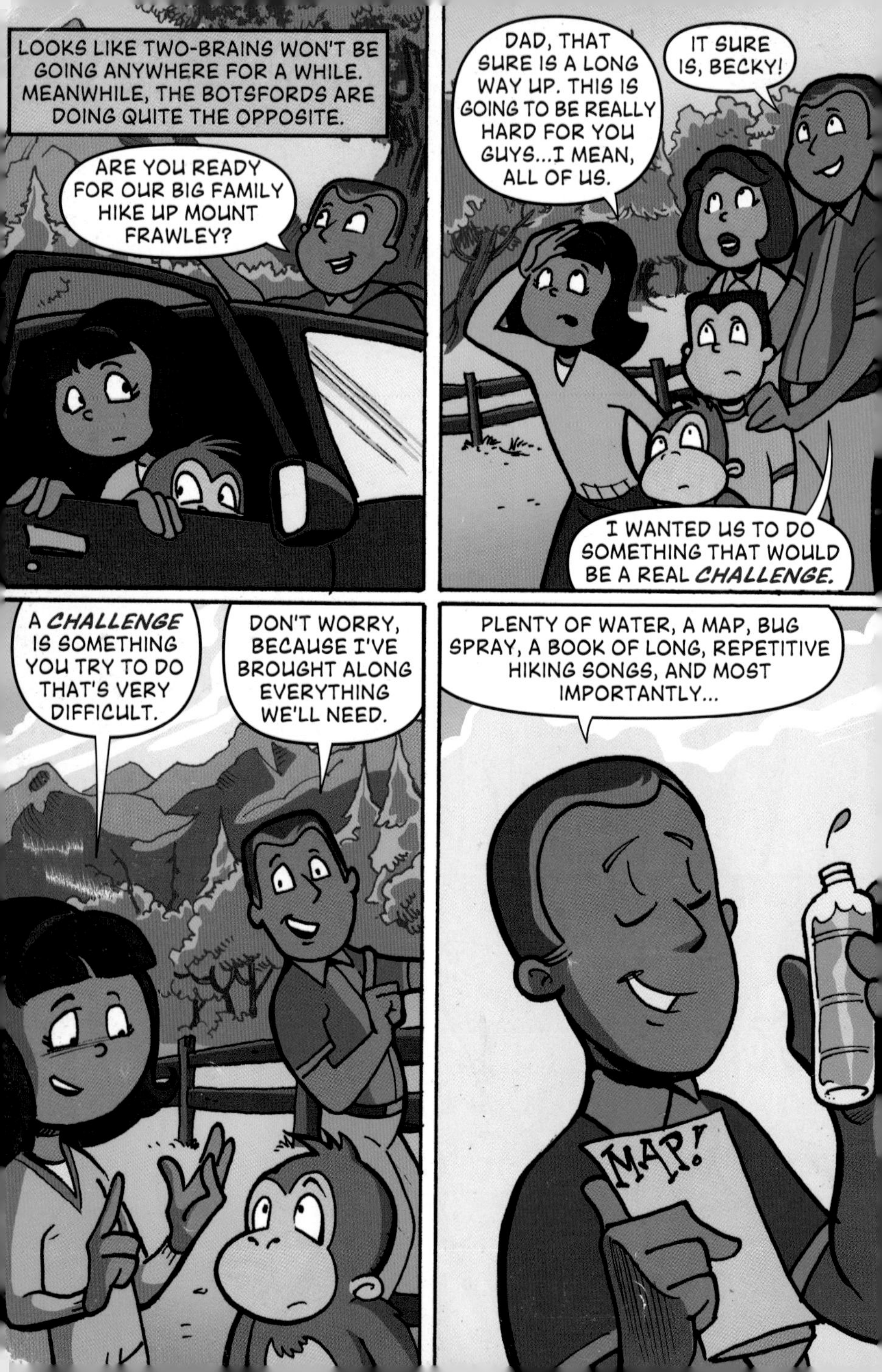
LOOKS LIKE TWO-BRAINS WON'T BE GOING ANYWHERE FOR A WHILE. MEANWHILE, THE BOTSFORDS ARE DOING QUITE THE OPPOSITE.
ARE YOU READY FOR OUR BIG FAMILY HIKE UP MOUNT FRAWLEY?
DAD, THAT SURE IS A LONG WAY UP. THIS IS GOING TO BE REALLY HARD FOR YOU GUYS...I MEAN, ALL OF US.
IT SURE IS, BECKY!
I WANTED US TO DO SOMETHING THAT WOULD BE A REAL *CHALLENGE.*
A *CHALLENGE* IS SOMETHING YOU TRY TO DO THAT'S VERY DIFFICULT.
DON'T WORRY, BECAUSE I'VE BROUGHT ALONG EVERYTHING WE'LL NEED.
PLENTY OF WATER, A MAP, BUG SPRAY, A BOOK OF LONG, REPETITIVE HIKING SONGS, AND MOST IMPORTANTLY...
MAP!

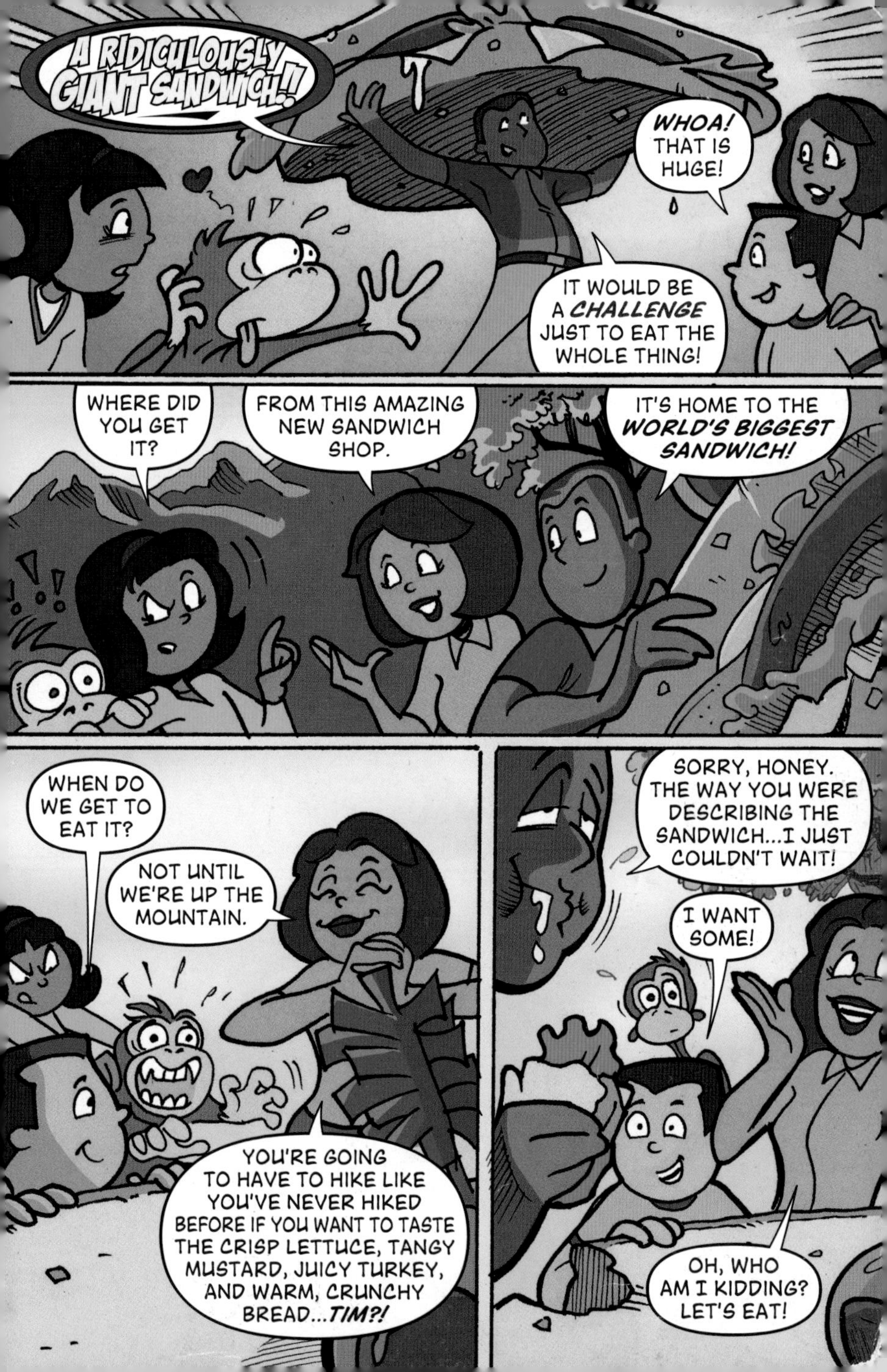
A RIDICULOUSLY GIANT SANDWICH!!
WHOA! THAT IS HUGE!
IT WOULD BE A CHALLENGE JUST TO EAT THE WHOLE THING!
WHERE DID YOU GET IT?
FROM THIS AMAZING NEW SANDWICH SHOP.
IT'S HOME TO THE WORLD'S BIGGEST SANDWICH!
WHEN DO WE GET TO EAT IT?
NOT UNTIL WE'RE UP THE MOUNTAIN.
YOU'RE GOING TO HAVE TO HIKE LIKE YOU'VE NEVER HIKED BEFORE IF YOU WANT TO TASTE THE CRISP LETTUCE, TANGY MUSTARD, JUICY TURKEY, AND WARM, CRUNCHY BREAD...TIM?!
SORRY, HONEY. THE WAY YOU WERE DESCRIBING THE SANDWICH...I JUST COULDN'T WAIT!
I WANT SOME!
OH, WHO AM I KIDDING? LET'S EAT!

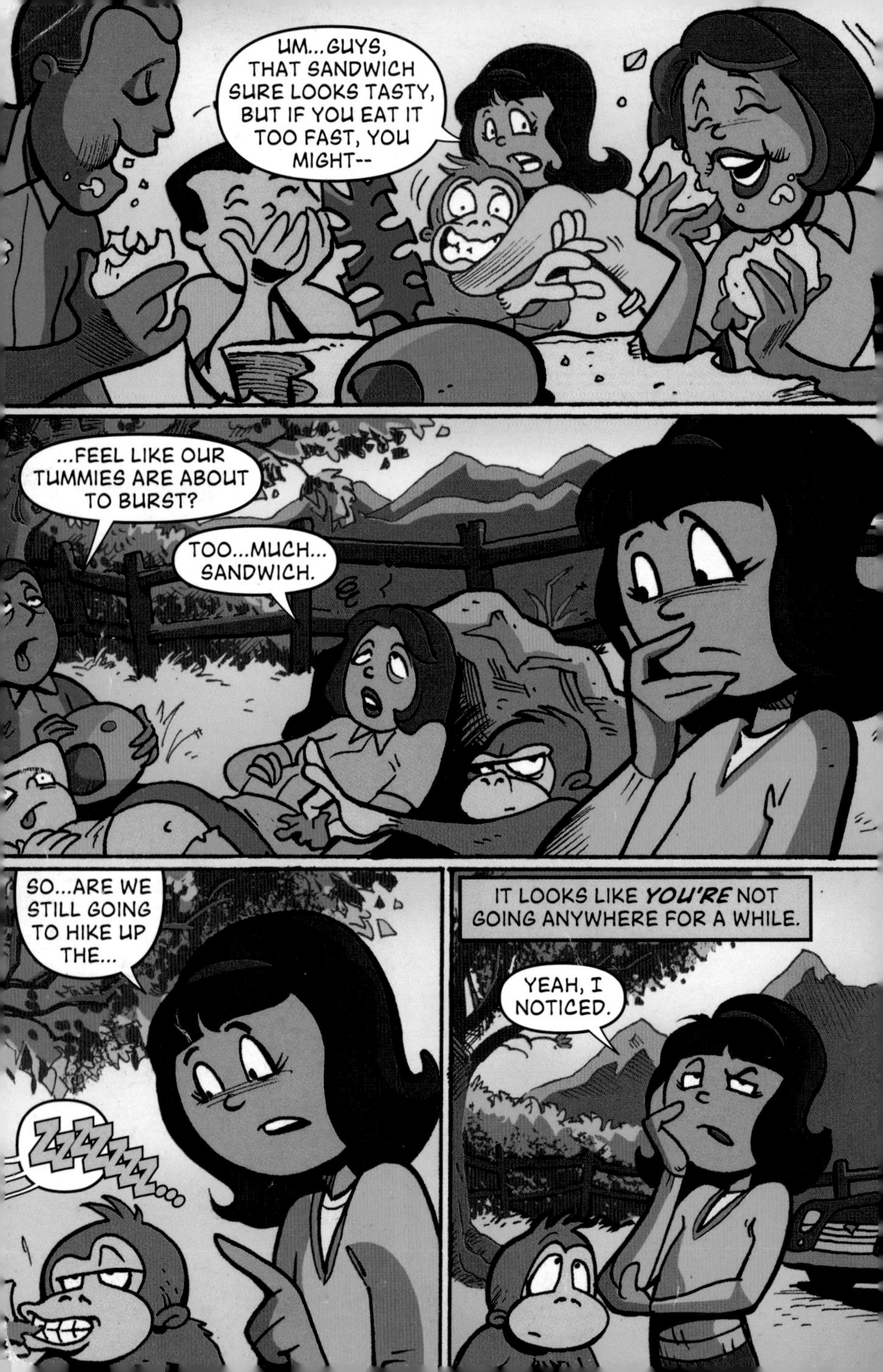
UM...GUYS, THAT SANDWICH SURE LOOKS TASTY, BUT IF YOU EAT IT TOO FAST, YOU MIGHT--
...FEEL LIKE OUR TUMMIES ARE ABOUT TO BURST?
TOO...MUCH... SANDWICH.
SO...ARE WE STILL GOING TO HIKE UP THE...
ZZZZZZZooo
IT LOOKS LIKE *YOU'RE* NOT GOING ANYWHERE FOR A WHILE.
YEAH, I NOTICED.

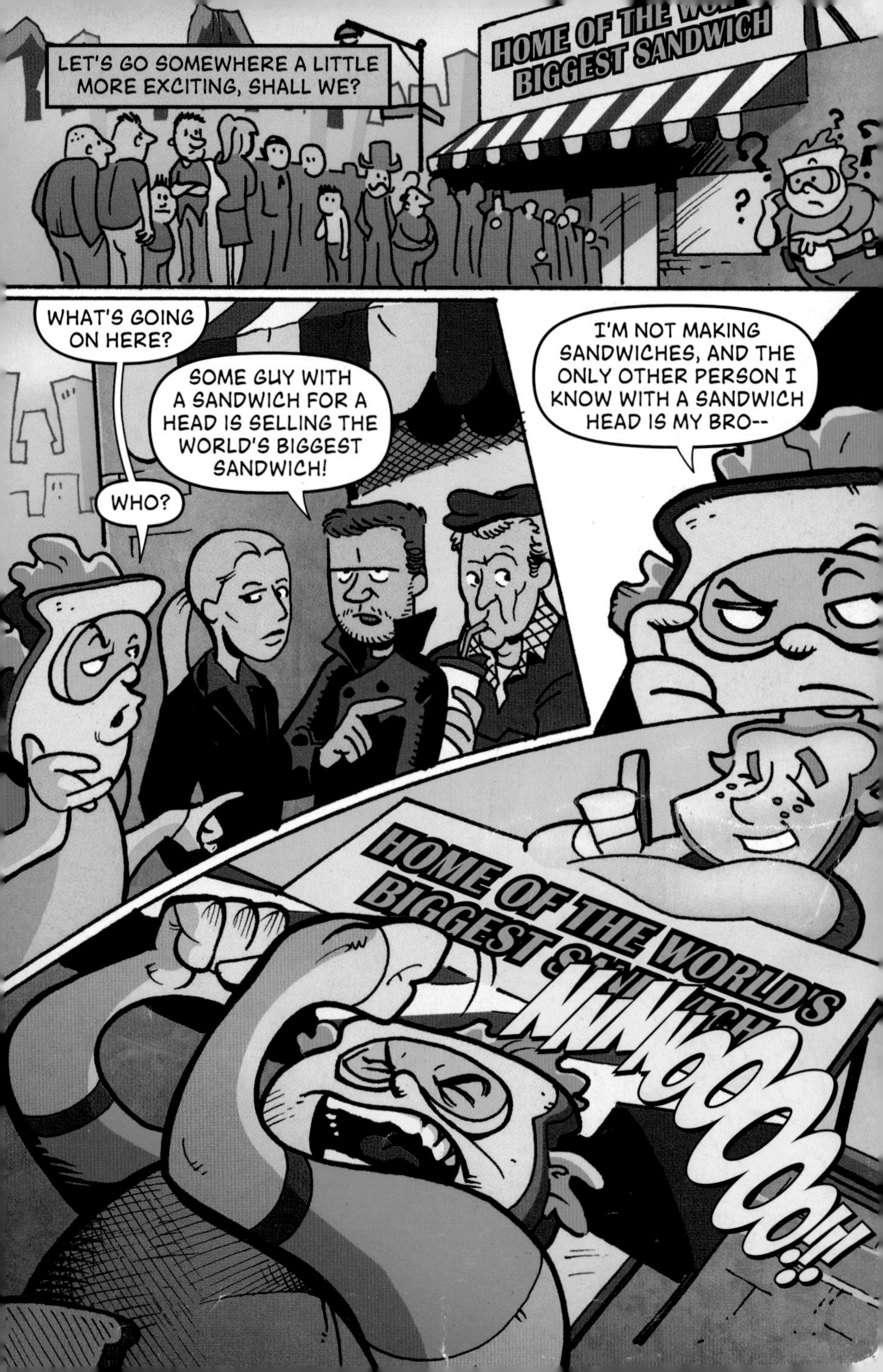
LET'S GO SOMEWHERE A LITTLE MORE EXCITING, SHALL WE?
HOME OF THE WO... BIGGEST SANDWICH
WHAT'S GOING ON HERE?
SOME GUY WITH A SANDWICH FOR A HEAD IS SELLING THE WORLD'S BIGGEST SANDWICH!
WHO?
I'M NOT MAKING SANDWICHES, AND THE ONLY OTHER PERSON I KNOW WITH A SANDWICH HEAD IS MY BRO--
HOME OF THE WORLD'S BIGGEST SANDWICH
NNNOOOOO!!

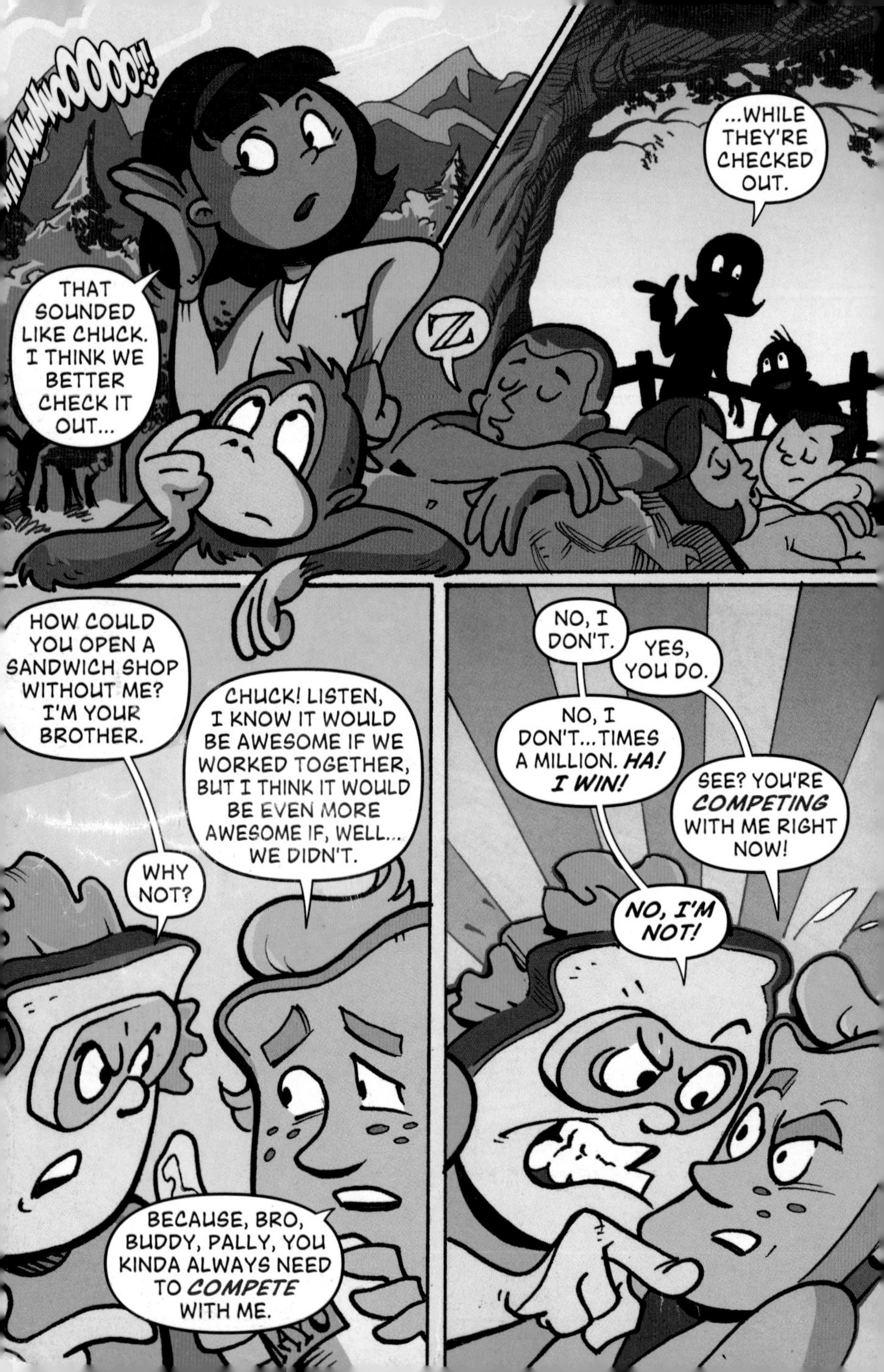

NNNNNNOOOOOO!!!
THAT SOUNDED LIKE CHUCK. I THINK WE BETTER CHECK IT OUT...
...WHILE THEY'RE CHECKED OUT.
Z
HOW COULD YOU OPEN A SANDWICH SHOP WITHOUT ME? I'M YOUR BROTHER.
CHUCK! LISTEN, I KNOW IT WOULD BE AWESOME IF WE WORKED TOGETHER, BUT I THINK IT WOULD BE EVEN MORE AWESOME IF, WELL... WE DIDN'T.
WHY NOT?
BECAUSE, BRO, BUDDY, PALLY, YOU KINDA ALWAYS NEED TO *COMPETE* WITH ME.
NO, I DON'T.
YES, YOU DO.
NO, I DON'T... TIMES A MILLION. ***HA! I WIN!***
SEE? YOU'RE *COMPETING* WITH ME RIGHT NOW!
NO, I'M NOT!

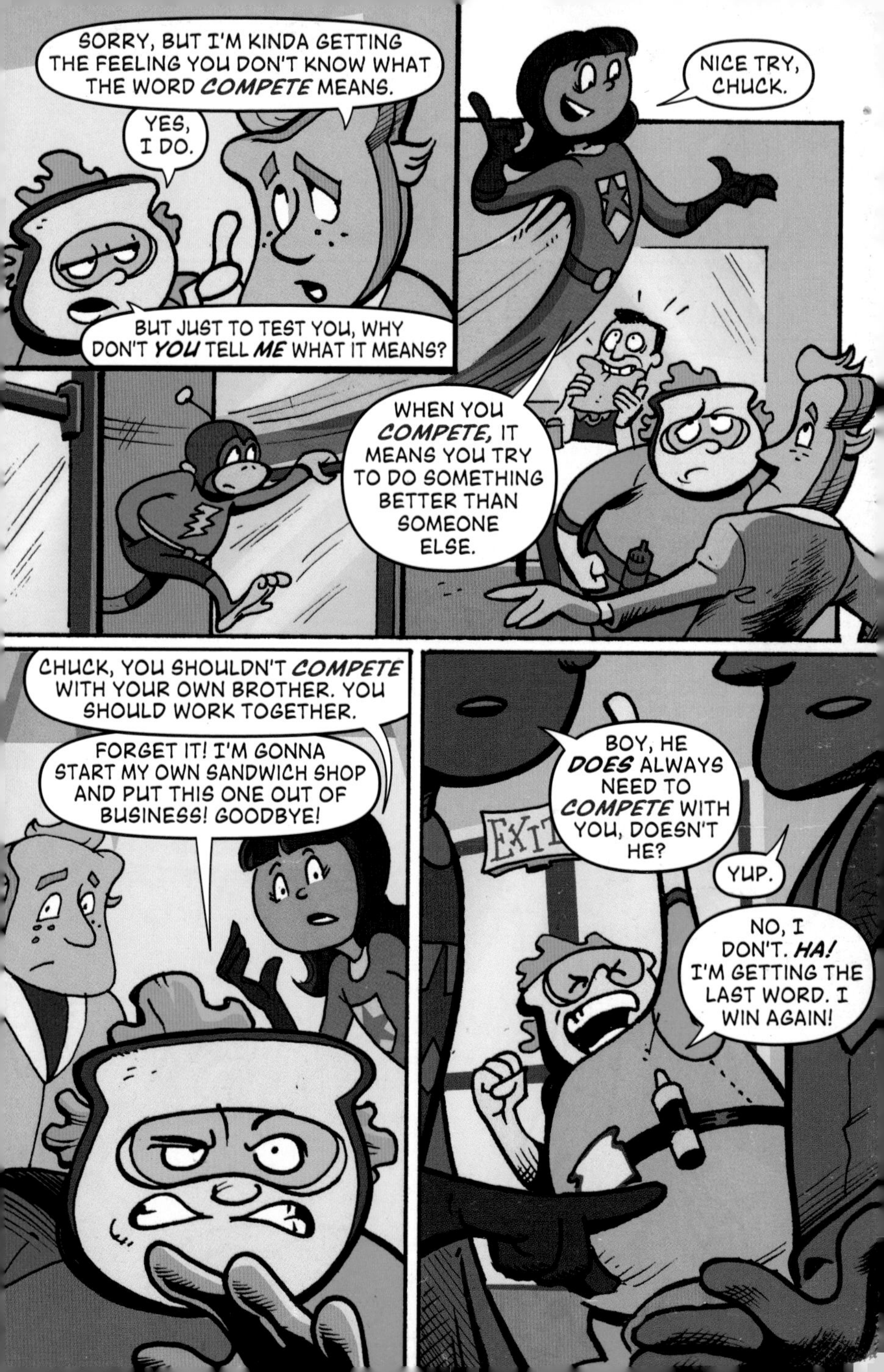
SORRY, BUT I'M KINDA GETTING THE FEELING YOU DON'T KNOW WHAT THE WORD COMPETE MEANS.
YES, I DO.
BUT JUST TO TEST YOU, WHY DON'T YOU TELL ME WHAT IT MEANS?
NICE TRY, CHUCK.
WHEN YOU COMPETE, IT MEANS YOU TRY TO DO SOMETHING BETTER THAN SOMEONE ELSE.
CHUCK, YOU SHOULDN'T COMPETE WITH YOUR OWN BROTHER. YOU SHOULD WORK TOGETHER.
FORGET IT! I'M GONNA START MY OWN SANDWICH SHOP AND PUT THIS ONE OUT OF BUSINESS! GOODBYE!
BOY, HE DOES ALWAYS NEED TO COMPETE WITH YOU, DOESN'T HE?
YUP.
NO, I DON'T. HA! I'M GETTING THE LAST WORD. I WIN AGAIN!

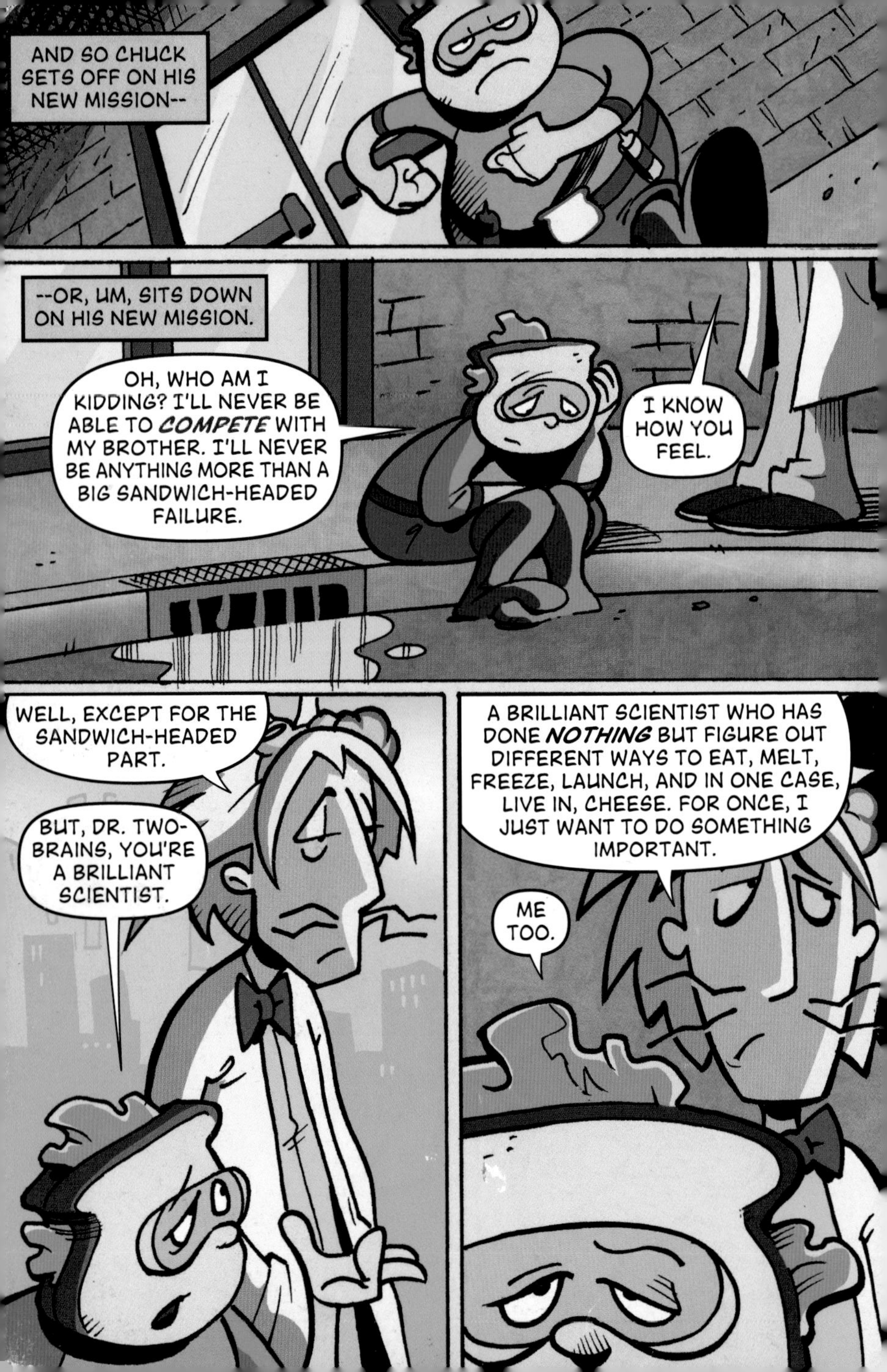
AND SO CHUCK SETS OFF ON HIS NEW MISSION--
--OR, UM, SITS DOWN ON HIS NEW MISSION.
OH, WHO AM I KIDDING? I'LL NEVER BE ABLE TO *COMPETE* WITH MY BROTHER. I'LL NEVER BE ANYTHING MORE THAN A BIG SANDWICH-HEADED FAILURE.
I KNOW HOW YOU FEEL.
WELL, EXCEPT FOR THE SANDWICH-HEADED PART.
BUT, DR. TWO-BRAINS, YOU'RE A BRILLIANT SCIENTIST.
A BRILLIANT SCIENTIST WHO HAS DONE *NOTHING* BUT FIGURE OUT DIFFERENT WAYS TO EAT, MELT, FREEZE, LAUNCH, AND IN ONE CASE, LIVE IN, CHEESE. FOR ONCE, I JUST WANT TO DO SOMETHING IMPORTANT.
ME TOO.

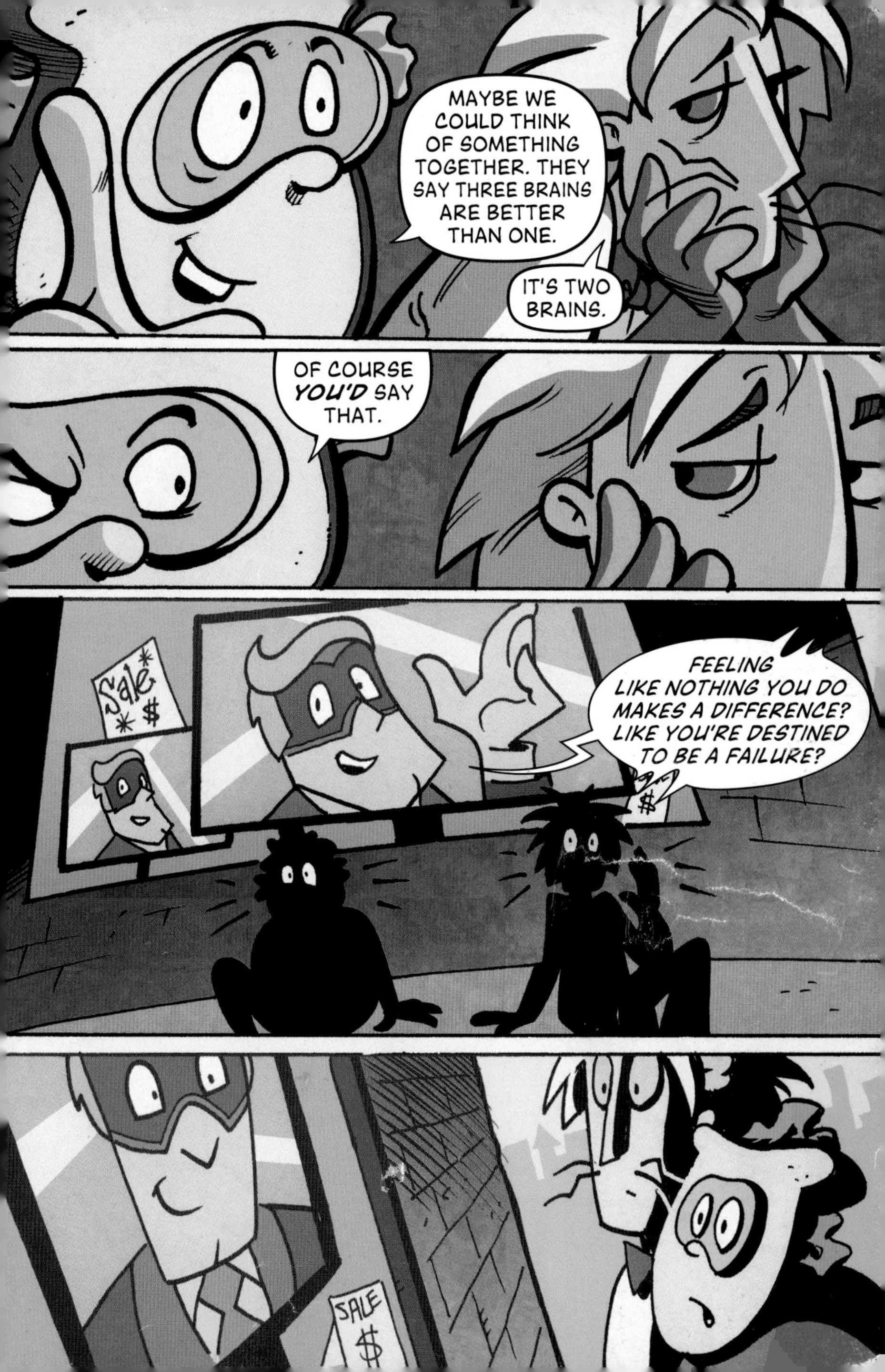
MAYBE WE COULD THINK OF SOMETHING TOGETHER. THEY SAY THREE BRAINS ARE BETTER THAN ONE.
IT'S TWO BRAINS.
OF COURSE *YOU'D* SAY THAT.
Sale $
FEELING LIKE NOTHING YOU DO MAKES A DIFFERENCE? LIKE YOU'RE DESTINED TO BE A FAILURE?
SALE $

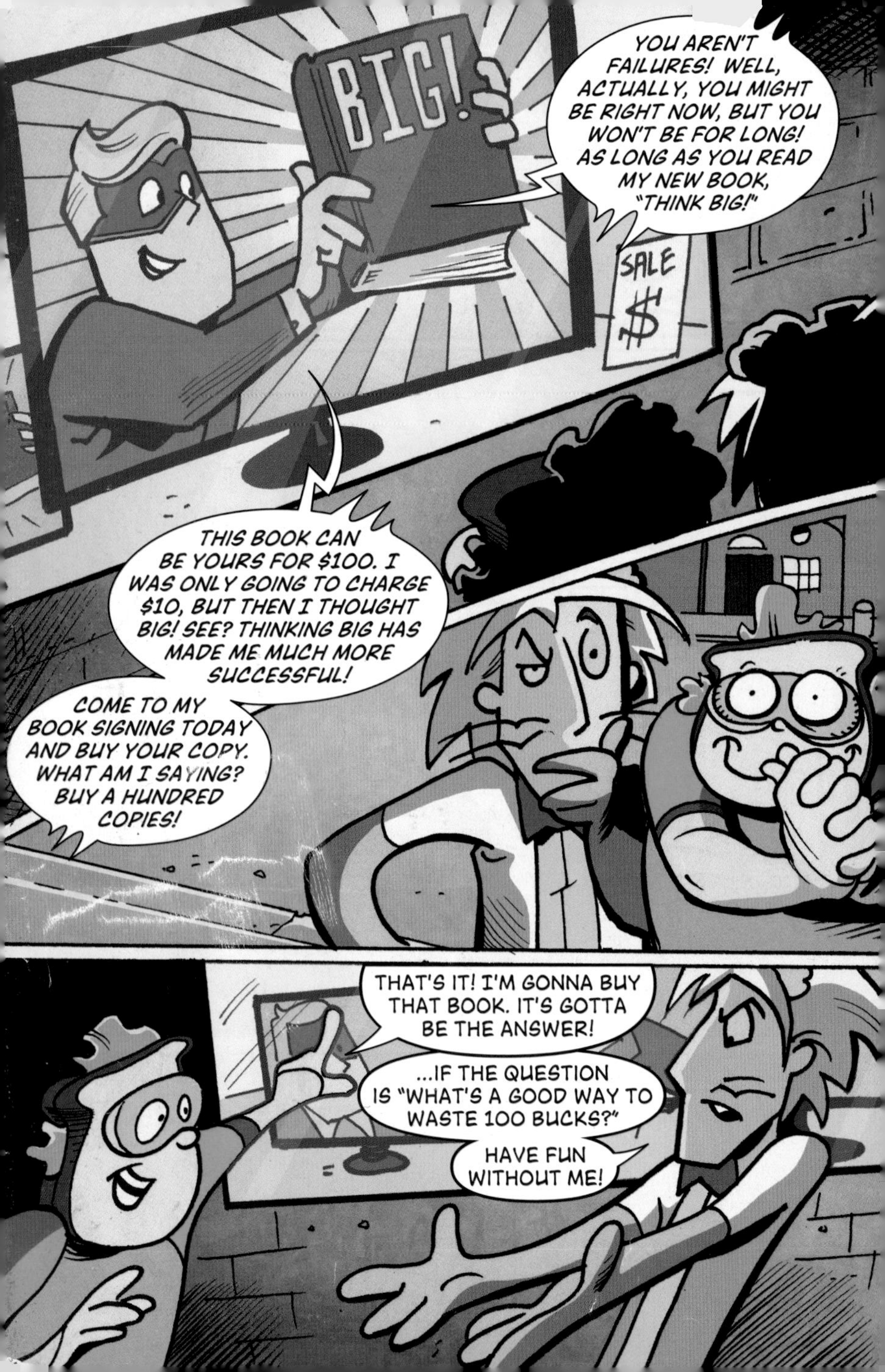
BIG!
YOU AREN'T FAILURES! WELL, ACTUALLY, YOU MIGHT BE RIGHT NOW, BUT YOU WON'T BE FOR LONG! AS LONG AS YOU READ MY NEW BOOK, "THINK BIG!"
SALE $
THIS BOOK CAN BE YOURS FOR $100. I WAS ONLY GOING TO CHARGE $10, BUT THEN I THOUGHT BIG! SEE? THINKING BIG HAS MADE ME MUCH MORE SUCCESSFUL!
COME TO MY BOOK SIGNING TODAY AND BUY YOUR COPY. WHAT AM I SAYING? BUY A HUNDRED COPIES!
THAT'S IT! I'M GONNA BUY THAT BOOK. IT'S GOTTA BE THE ANSWER!
...IF THE QUESTION IS "WHAT'S A GOOD WAY TO WASTE 100 BUCKS?"
HAVE FUN WITHOUT ME!

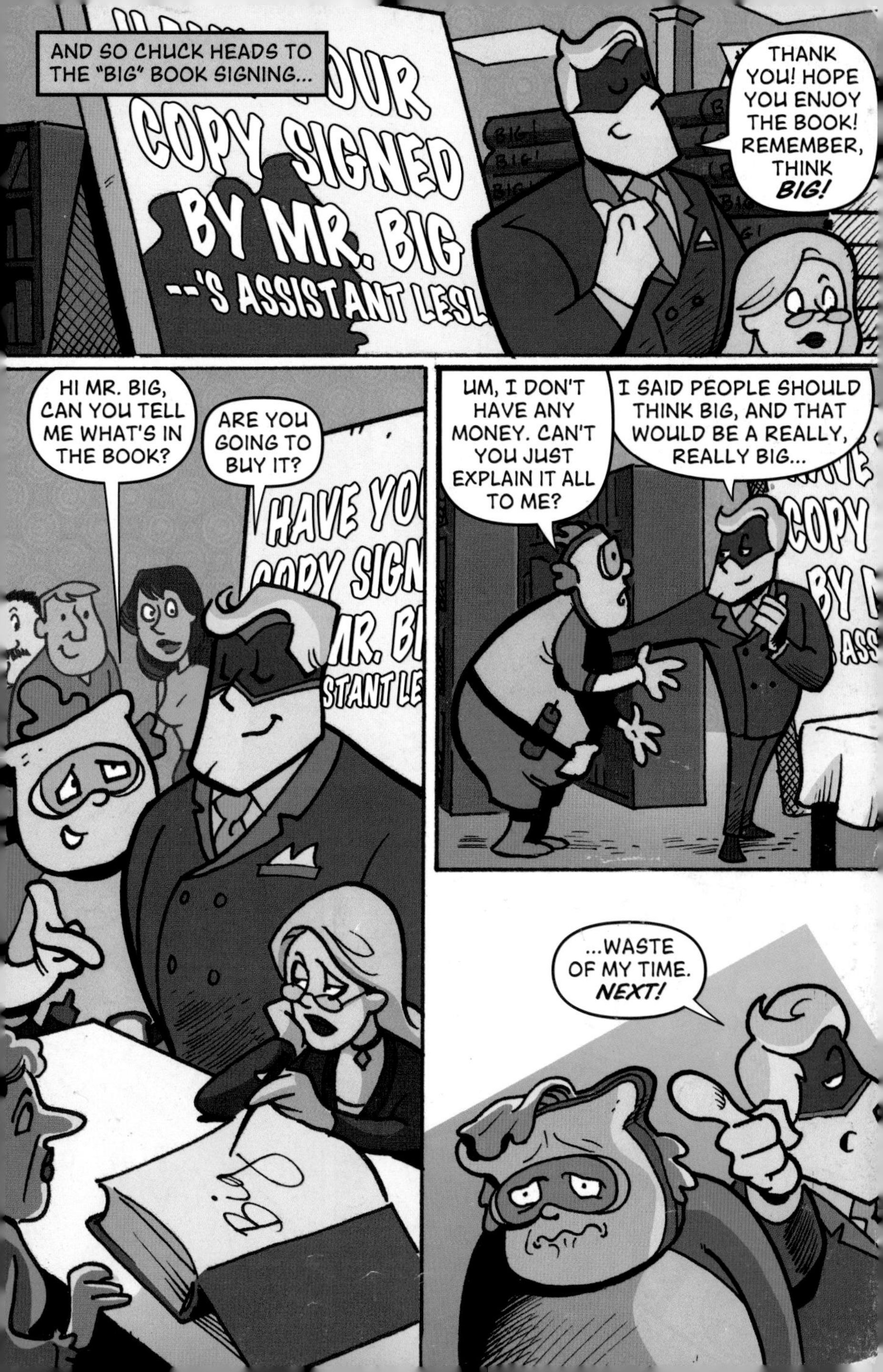
AND SO CHUCK HEADS TO THE "BIG" BOOK SIGNING...
COPY SIGNED BY MR. BIG --'S ASSISTANT LESL
THANK YOU! HOPE YOU ENJOY THE BOOK! REMEMBER, THINK *BIG!*
HI MR. BIG, CAN YOU TELL ME WHAT'S IN THE BOOK?
ARE YOU GOING TO BUY IT?
UM, I DON'T HAVE ANY MONEY. CAN'T YOU JUST EXPLAIN IT ALL TO ME?
I SAID PEOPLE SHOULD THINK BIG, AND THAT WOULD BE A REALLY, REALLY BIG...
...WASTE OF MY TIME. *NEXT!*

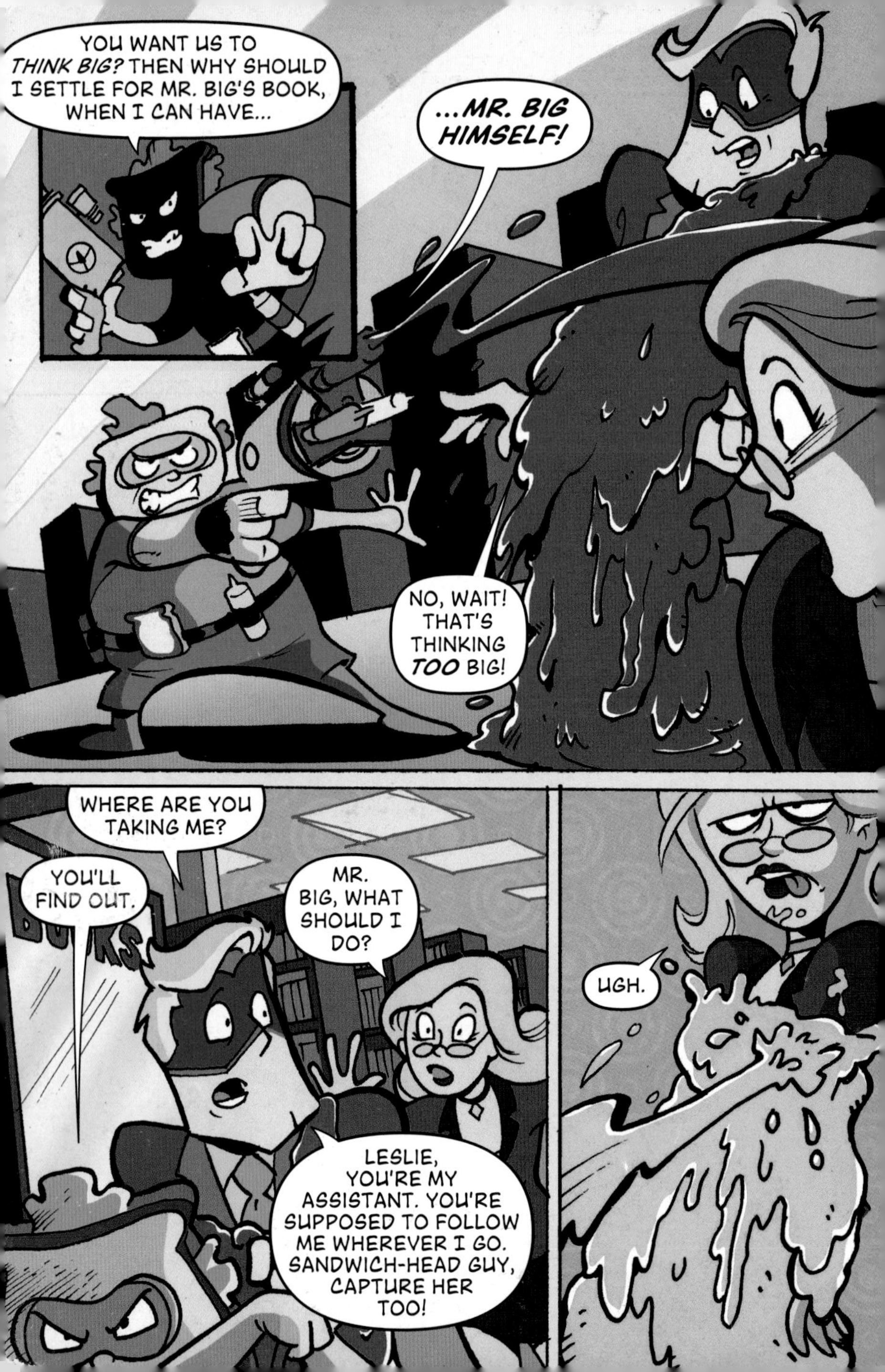
YOU WANT US TO *THINK BIG?* THEN WHY SHOULD I SETTLE FOR MR. BIG'S BOOK, WHEN I CAN HAVE...
...MR. BIG HIMSELF!
NO, WAIT! THAT'S THINKING *TOO* BIG!
WHERE ARE YOU TAKING ME?
YOU'LL FIND OUT.
MR. BIG, WHAT SHOULD I DO?
LESLIE, YOU'RE MY ASSISTANT. YOU'RE SUPPOSED TO FOLLOW ME WHEREVER I GO. SANDWICH-HEAD GUY, CAPTURE HER TOO!
UGH.

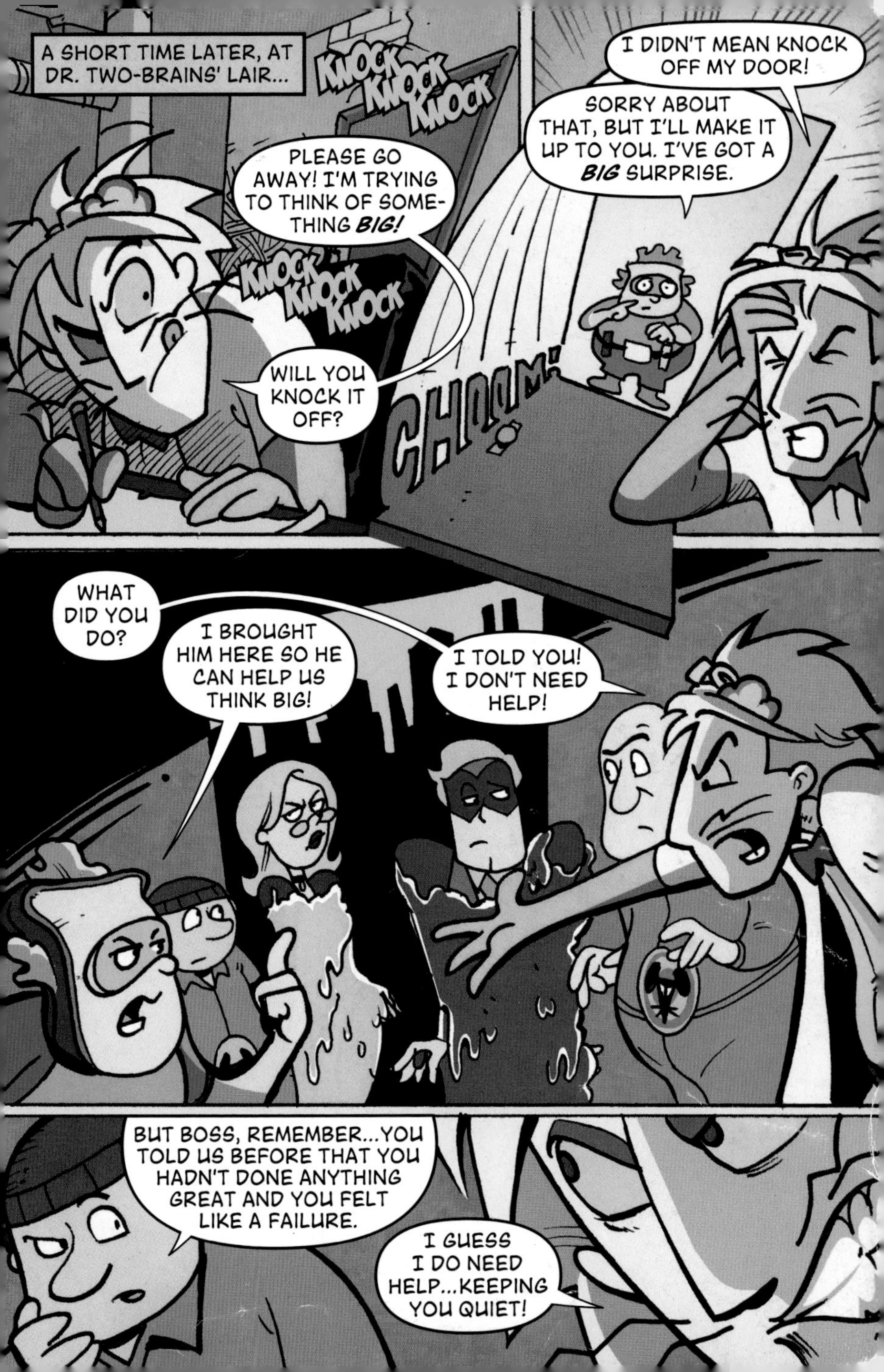
A SHORT TIME LATER, AT DR. TWO-BRAINS' LAIR...
KNOCK KNOCK KNOCK
PLEASE GO AWAY! I'M TRYING TO THINK OF SOME-THING *BIG!*
KNOCK KNOCK KNOCK
WILL YOU KNOCK IT OFF?
CHOOM!
I DIDN'T MEAN KNOCK OFF MY DOOR!
SORRY ABOUT THAT, BUT I'LL MAKE IT UP TO YOU. I'VE GOT A *BIG* SURPRISE.
WHAT DID YOU DO?
I BROUGHT HIM HERE SO HE CAN HELP US THINK BIG!
I TOLD YOU! I DON'T NEED HELP!
BUT BOSS, REMEMBER...YOU TOLD US BEFORE THAT YOU HADN'T DONE ANYTHING GREAT AND YOU FELT LIKE A FAILURE.
I GUESS I DO NEED HELP...KEEPING YOU QUIET!

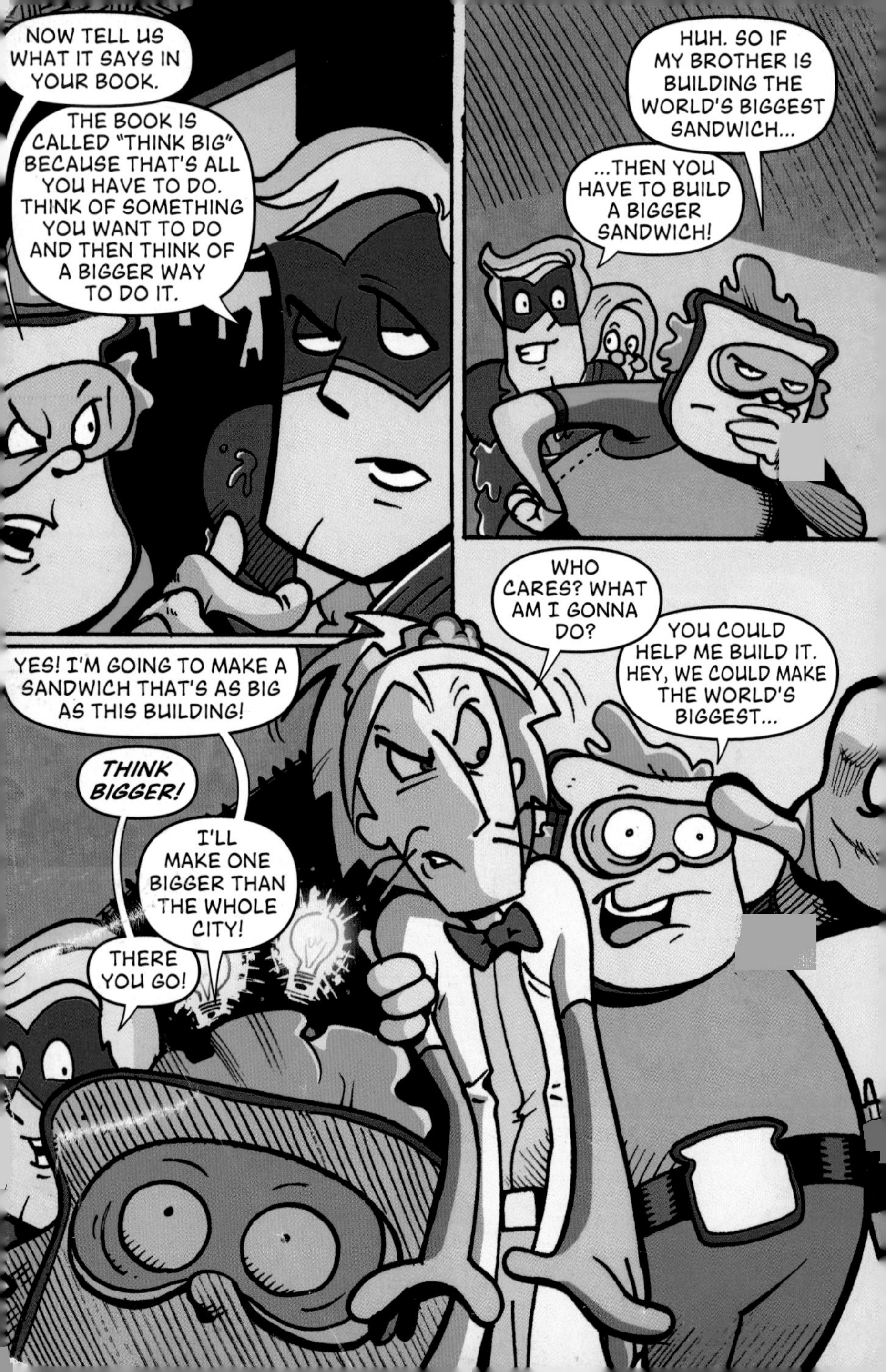
NOW TELL US WHAT IT SAYS IN YOUR BOOK.
THE BOOK IS CALLED "THINK BIG" BECAUSE THAT'S ALL YOU HAVE TO DO. THINK OF SOMETHING YOU WANT TO DO AND THEN THINK OF A BIGGER WAY TO DO IT.
HUH. SO IF MY BROTHER IS BUILDING THE WORLD'S BIGGEST SANDWICH...
...THEN YOU HAVE TO BUILD A BIGGER SANDWICH!
YES! I'M GOING TO MAKE A SANDWICH THAT'S AS BIG AS THIS BUILDING!
THINK BIGGER!
I'LL MAKE ONE BIGGER THAN THE WHOLE CITY!
THERE YOU GO!
WHO CARES? WHAT AM I GONNA DO?
YOU COULD HELP ME BUILD IT. HEY, WE COULD MAKE THE WORLD'S BIGGEST...

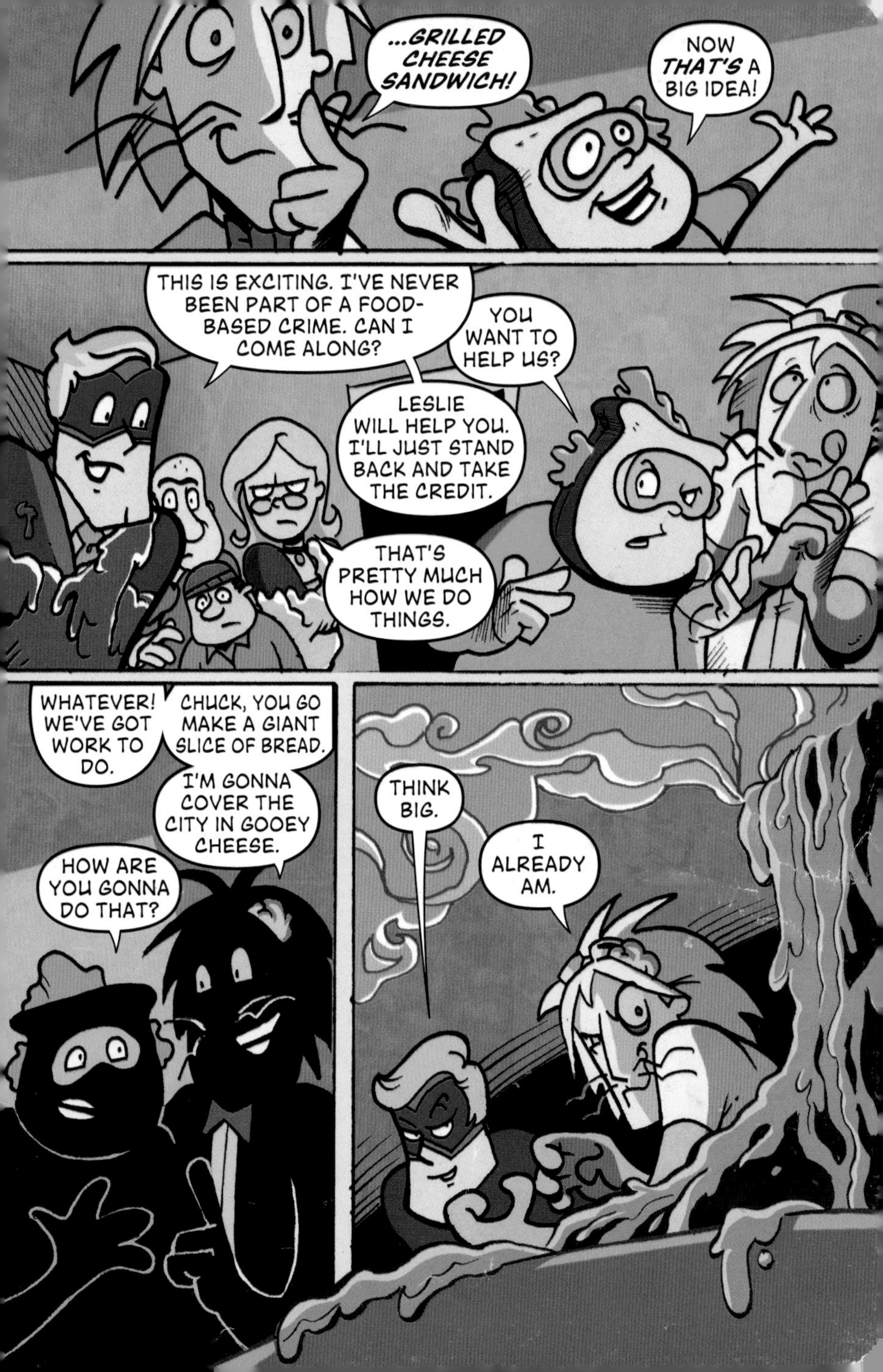
...GRILLED CHEESE SANDWICH!
NOW THAT'S A BIG IDEA!
THIS IS EXCITING. I'VE NEVER BEEN PART OF A FOOD-BASED CRIME. CAN I COME ALONG?
YOU WANT TO HELP US?
LESLIE WILL HELP YOU. I'LL JUST STAND BACK AND TAKE THE CREDIT.
THAT'S PRETTY MUCH HOW WE DO THINGS.
WHATEVER! WE'VE GOT WORK TO DO.
CHUCK, YOU GO MAKE A GIANT SLICE OF BREAD.
I'M GONNA COVER THE CITY IN GOOEY CHEESE.
HOW ARE YOU GONNA DO THAT?
THINK BIG.
I ALREADY AM.

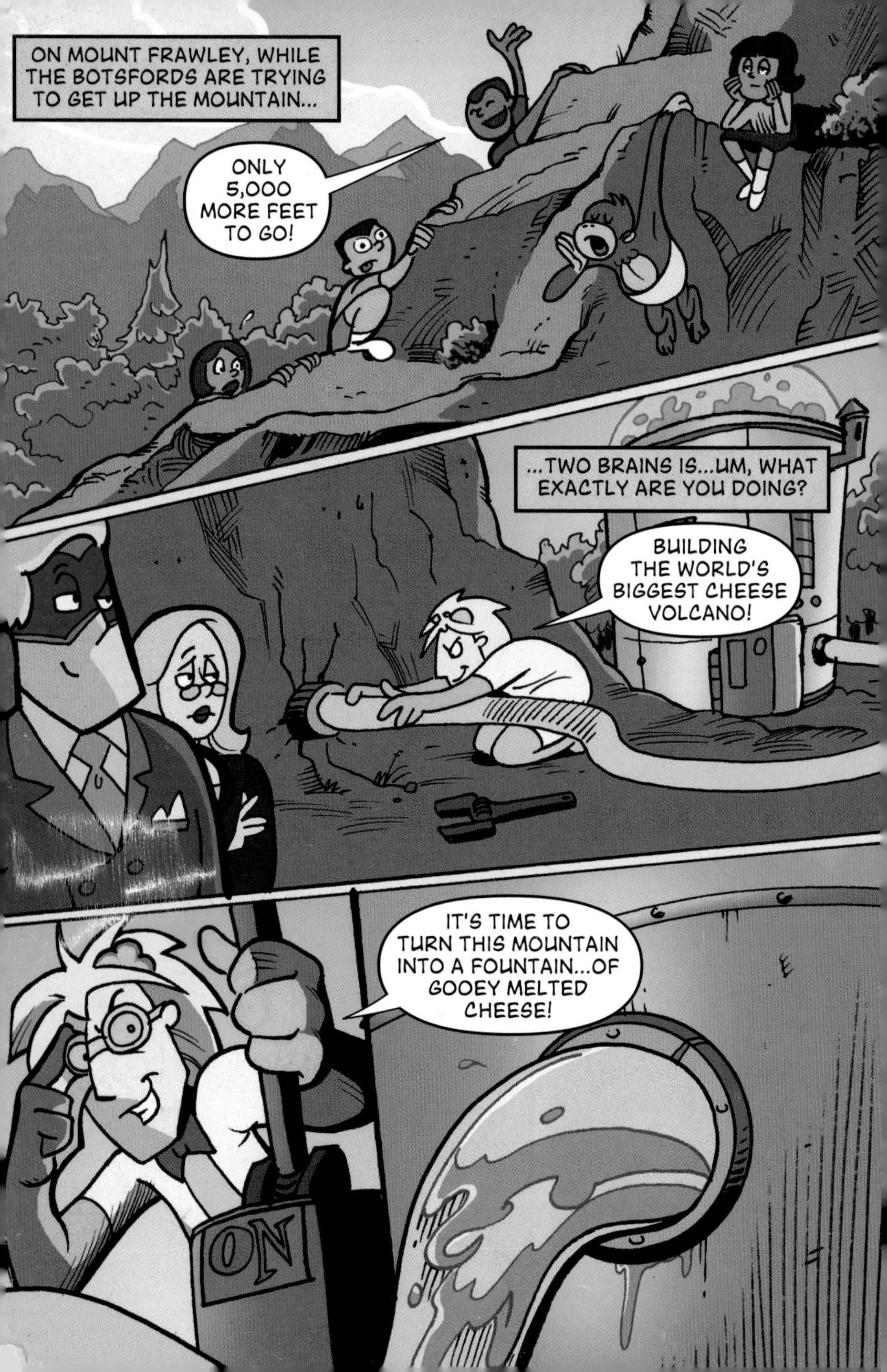
ON MOUNT FRAWLEY, WHILE THE BOTSFORDS ARE TRYING TO GET UP THE MOUNTAIN...
ONLY 5,000 MORE FEET TO GO!
...TWO BRAINS IS...UM, WHAT EXACTLY ARE YOU DOING?
BUILDING THE WORLD'S BIGGEST CHEESE VOLCANO!
IT'S TIME TO TURN THIS MOUNTAIN INTO A FOUNTAIN...OF GOOEY MELTED CHEESE!
ON

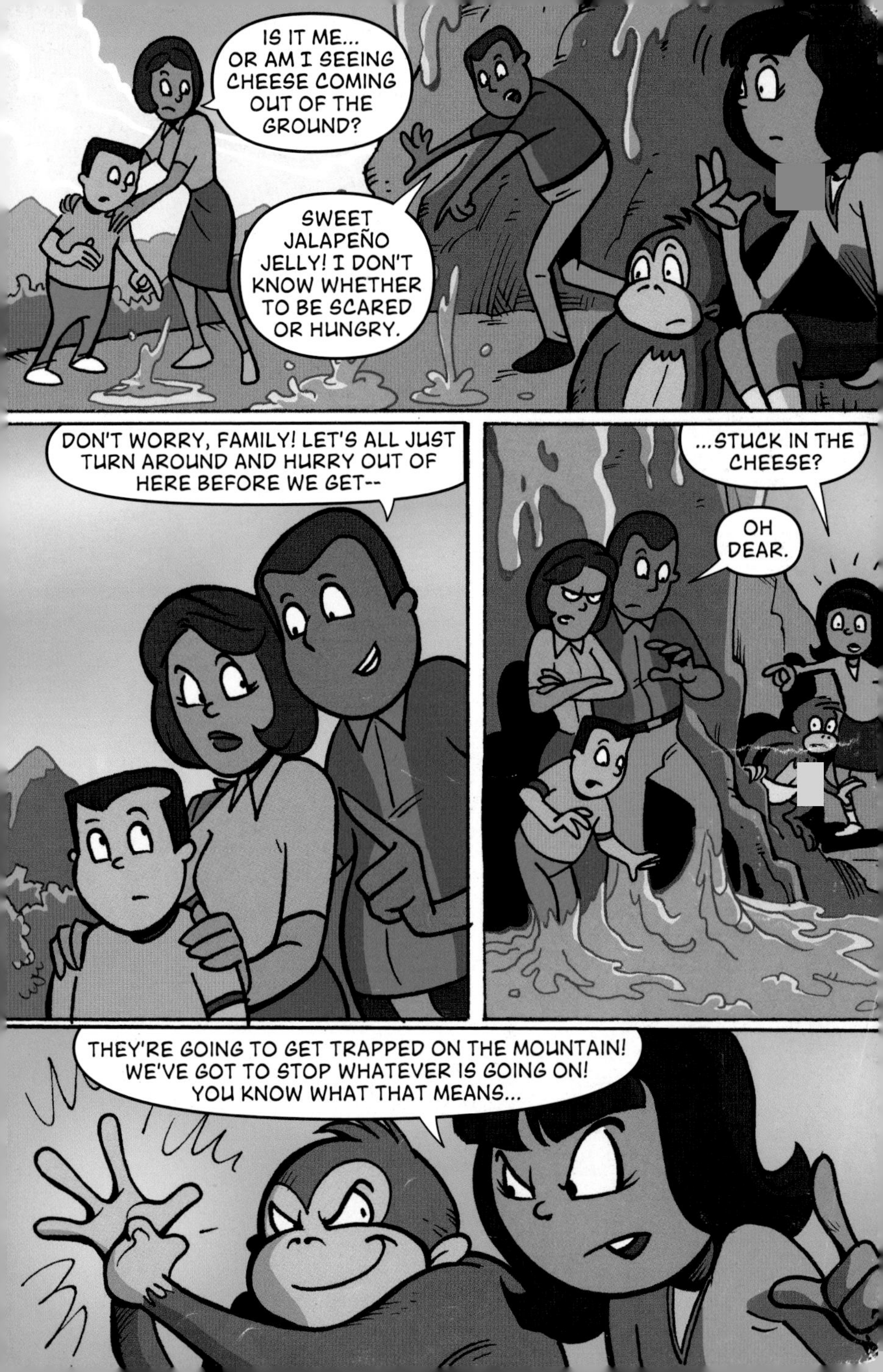
IS IT ME... OR AM I SEEING CHEESE COMING OUT OF THE GROUND?
SWEET JALAPEÑO JELLY! I DON'T KNOW WHETHER TO BE SCARED OR HUNGRY.
DON'T WORRY, FAMILY! LET'S ALL JUST TURN AROUND AND HURRY OUT OF HERE BEFORE WE GET--
...STUCK IN THE CHEESE?
OH DEAR.
THEY'RE GOING TO GET TRAPPED ON THE MOUNTAIN! WE'VE GOT TO STOP WHATEVER IS GOING ON! YOU KNOW WHAT THAT MEANS...

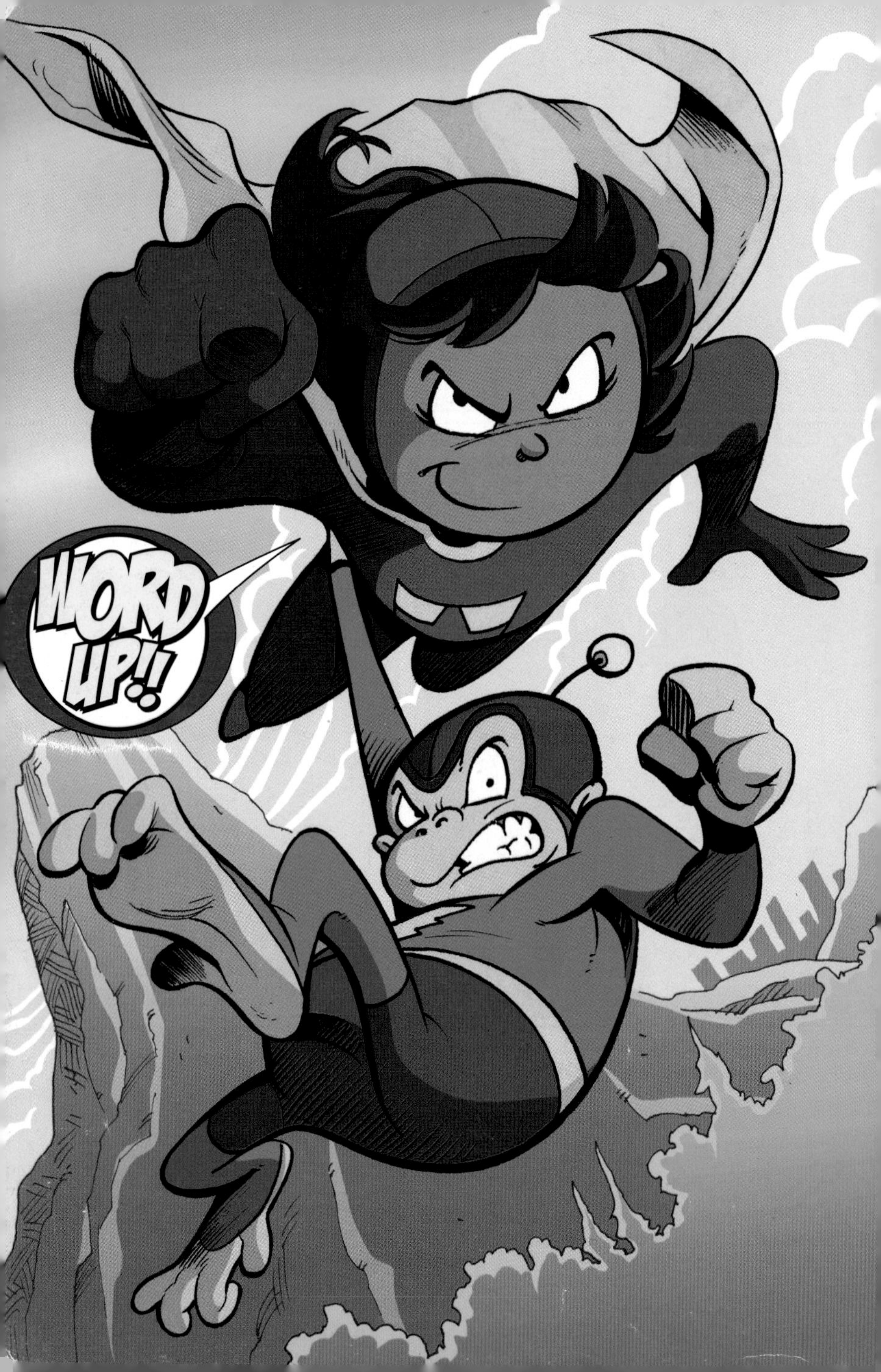
WORD UP!!

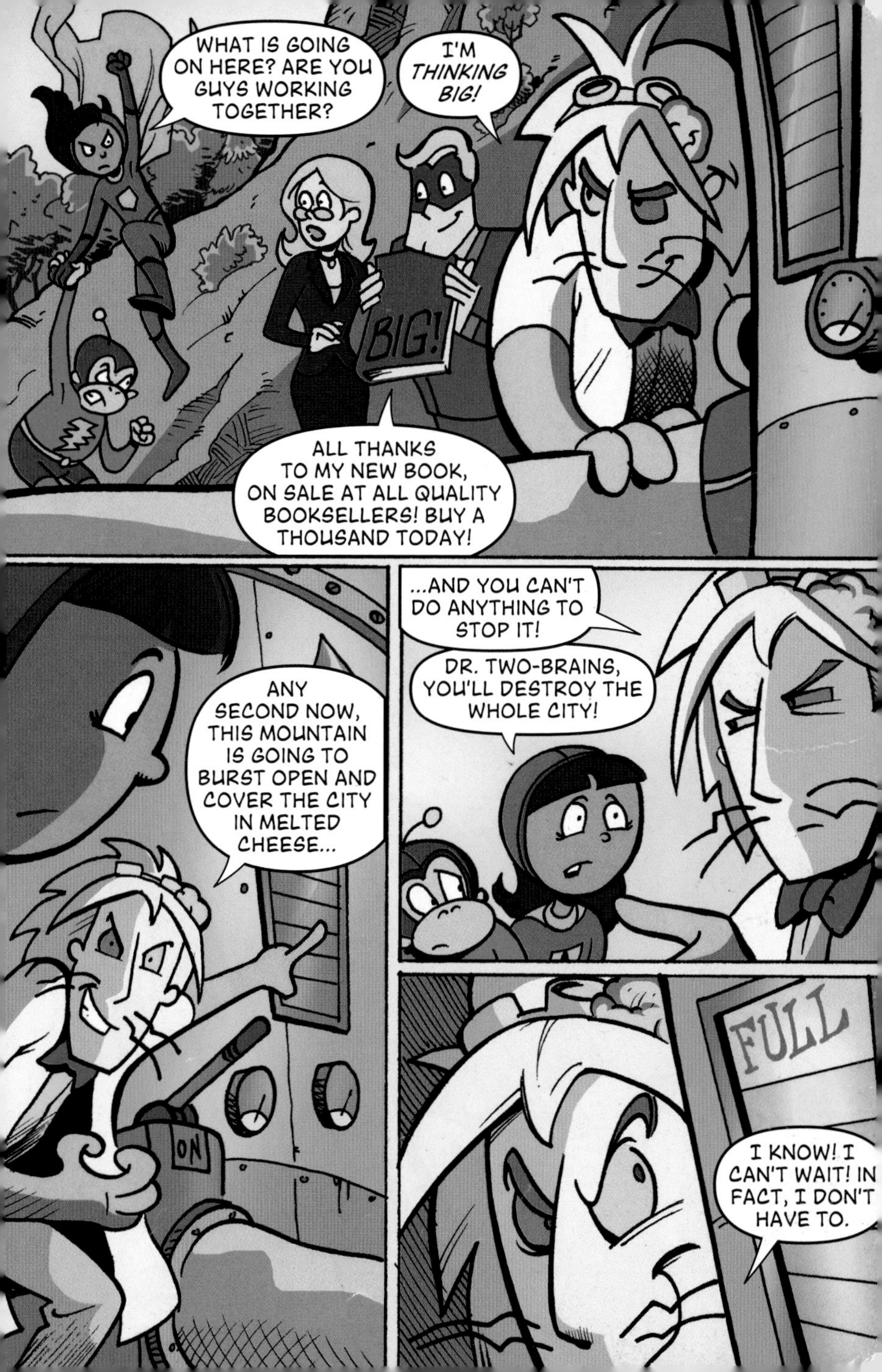
WHAT IS GOING ON HERE? ARE YOU GUYS WORKING TOGETHER?
I'M *THINKING BIG!*
BIG!
ALL THANKS TO MY NEW BOOK, ON SALE AT ALL QUALITY BOOKSELLERS! BUY A THOUSAND TODAY!
ANY SECOND NOW, THIS MOUNTAIN IS GOING TO BURST OPEN AND COVER THE CITY IN MELTED CHEESE...
ON
...AND YOU CAN'T DO ANYTHING TO STOP IT!
DR. TWO-BRAINS, YOU'LL DESTROY THE WHOLE CITY!
FULL
I KNOW! I CAN'T WAIT! IN FACT, I DON'T HAVE TO.

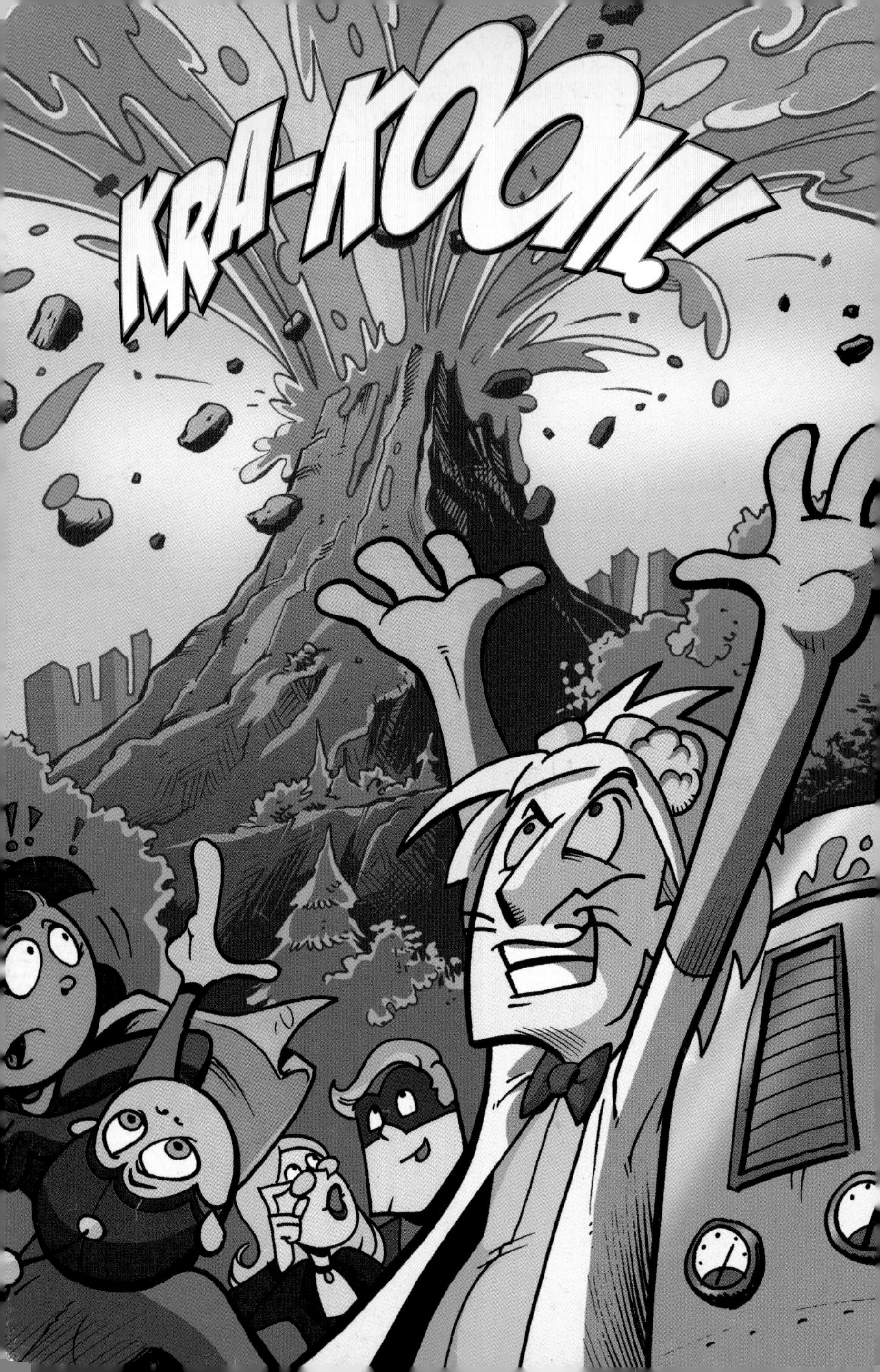
KRA-KOOM!
!!
!

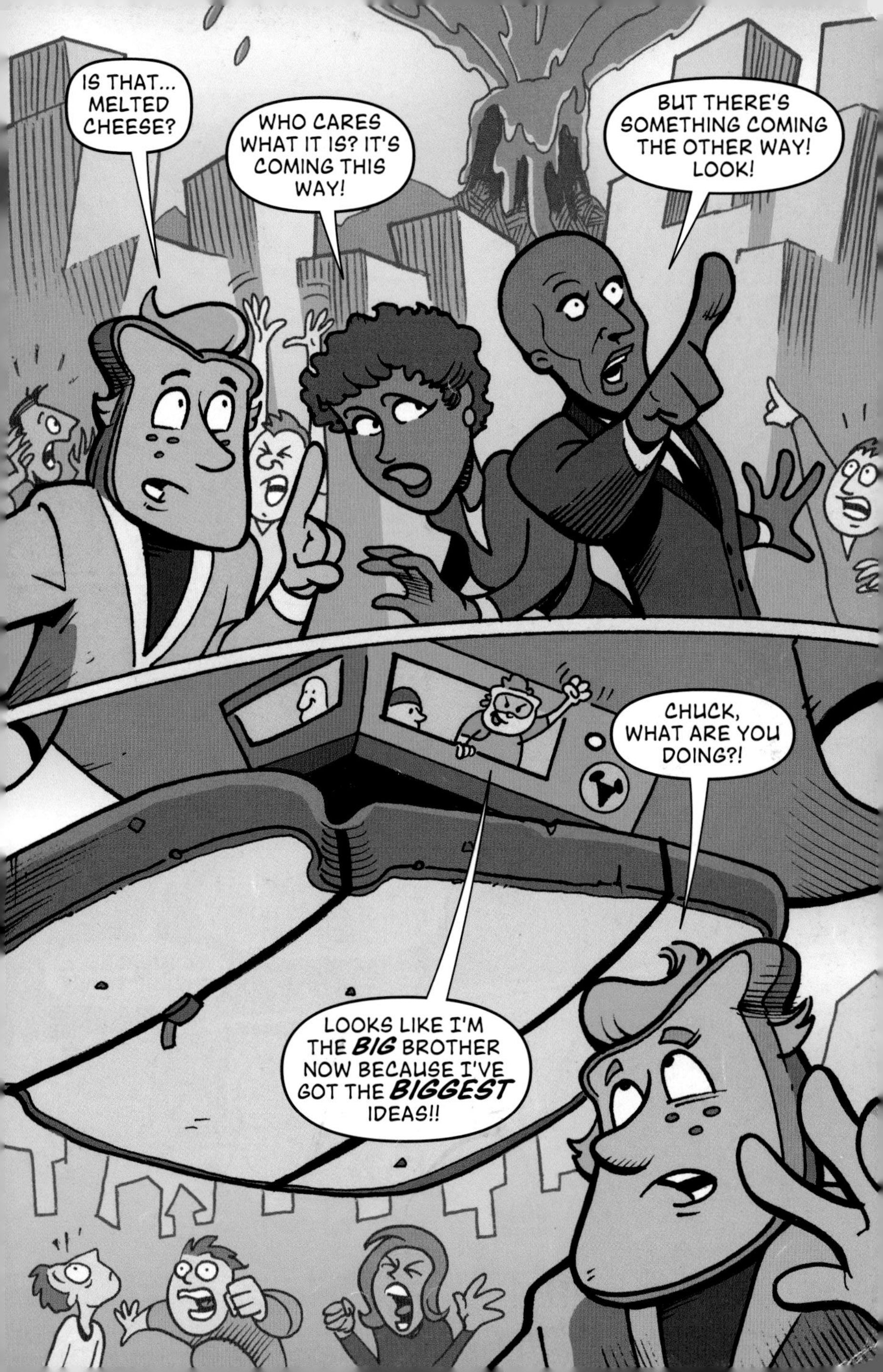
IS THAT... MELTED CHEESE?
WHO CARES WHAT IT IS? IT'S COMING THIS WAY!
BUT THERE'S SOMETHING COMING THE OTHER WAY! LOOK!
CHUCK, WHAT ARE YOU DOING?!
LOOKS LIKE I'M THE *BIG* BROTHER NOW BECAUSE I'VE GOT THE *BIGGEST* IDEAS!!

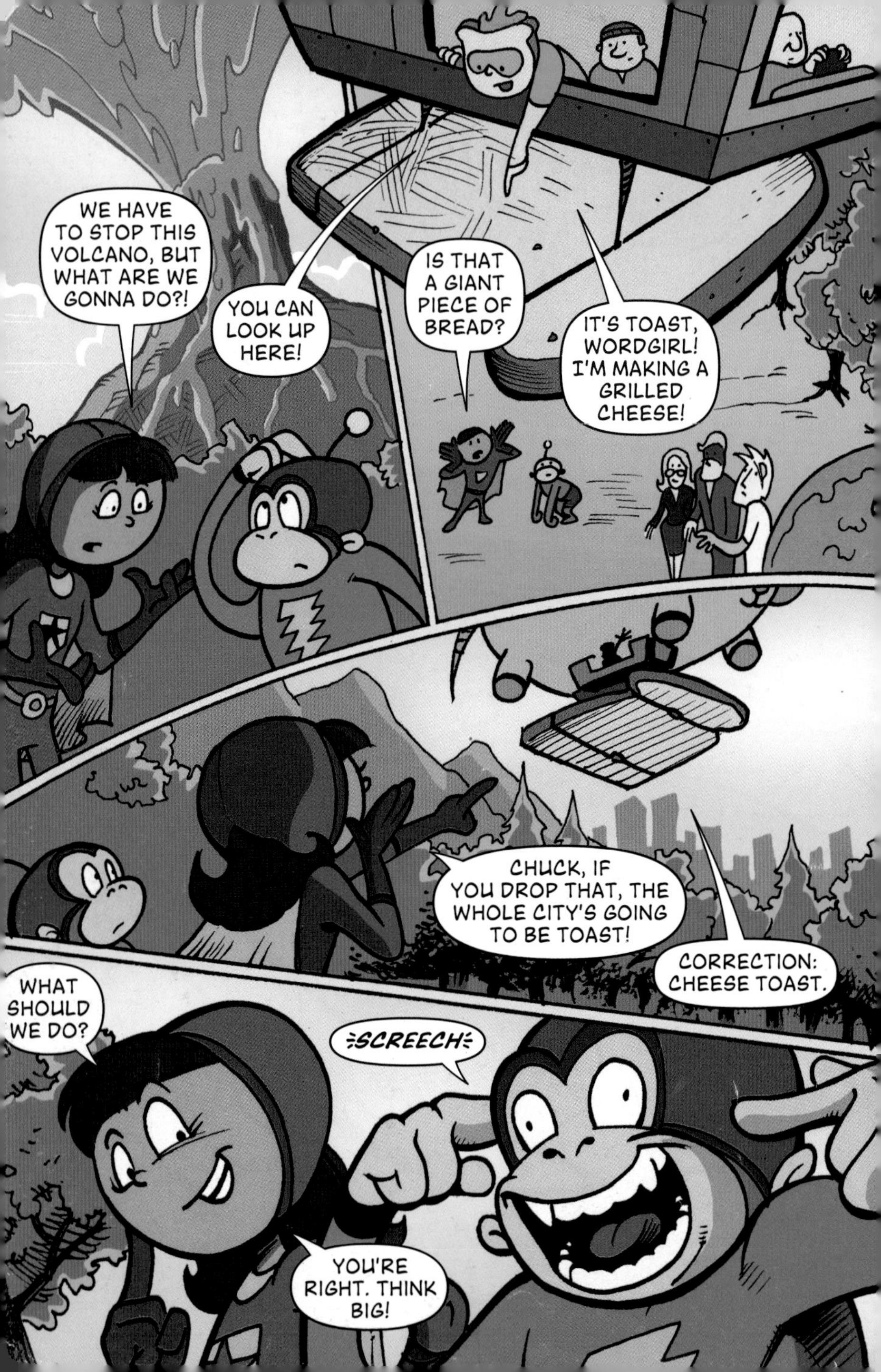
WE HAVE TO STOP THIS VOLCANO, BUT WHAT ARE WE GONNA DO?!
YOU CAN LOOK UP HERE!
IS THAT A GIANT PIECE OF BREAD?
IT'S TOAST, WORDGIRL! I'M MAKING A GRILLED CHEESE!
CHUCK, IF YOU DROP THAT, THE WHOLE CITY'S GOING TO BE TOAST!
CORRECTION: CHEESE TOAST.
WHAT SHOULD WE DO?
SCREECH
YOU'RE RIGHT. THINK BIG!

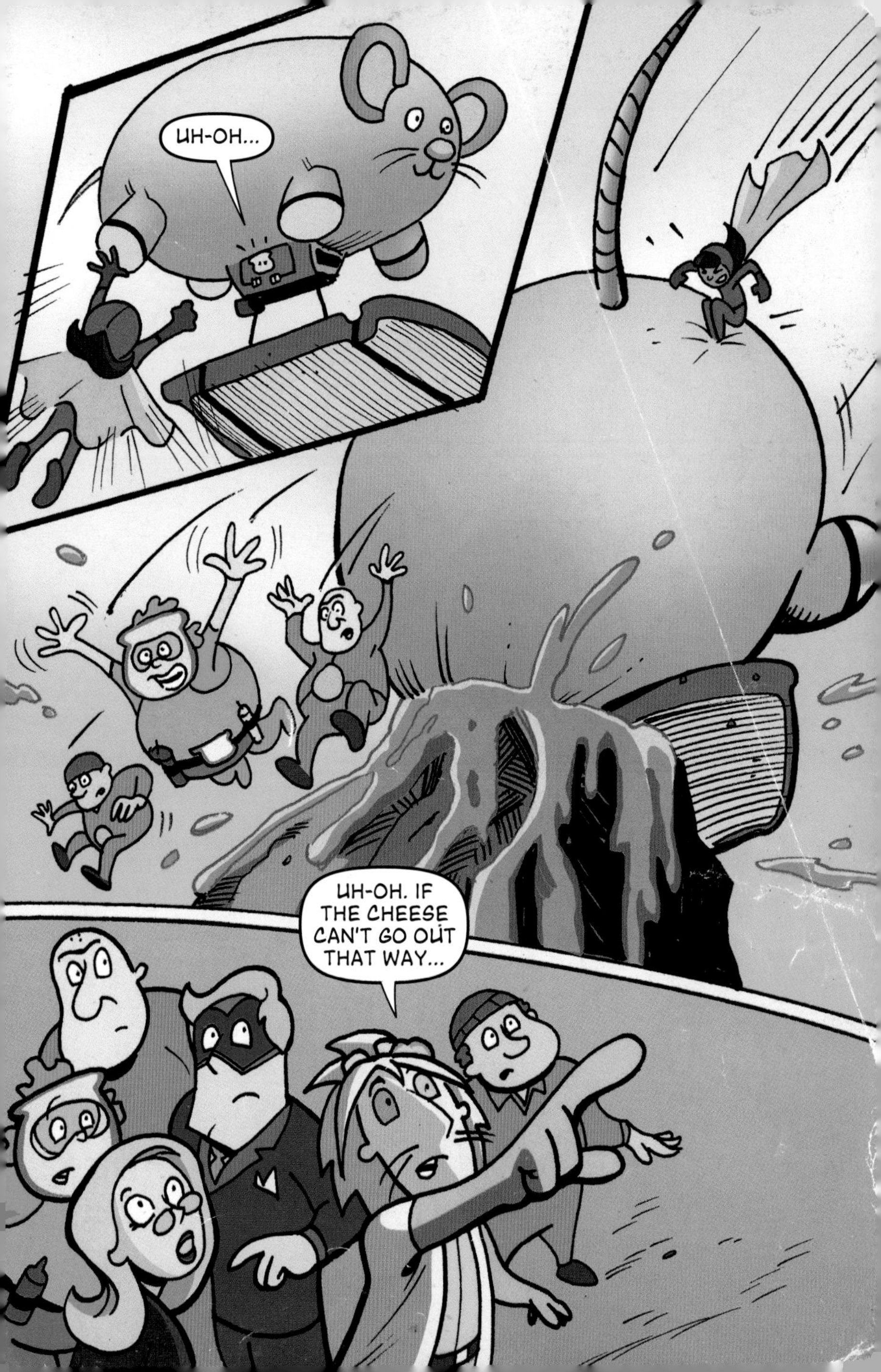
UH-OH...
UH-OH. IF THE CHEESE CAN'T GO OUT THAT WAY...

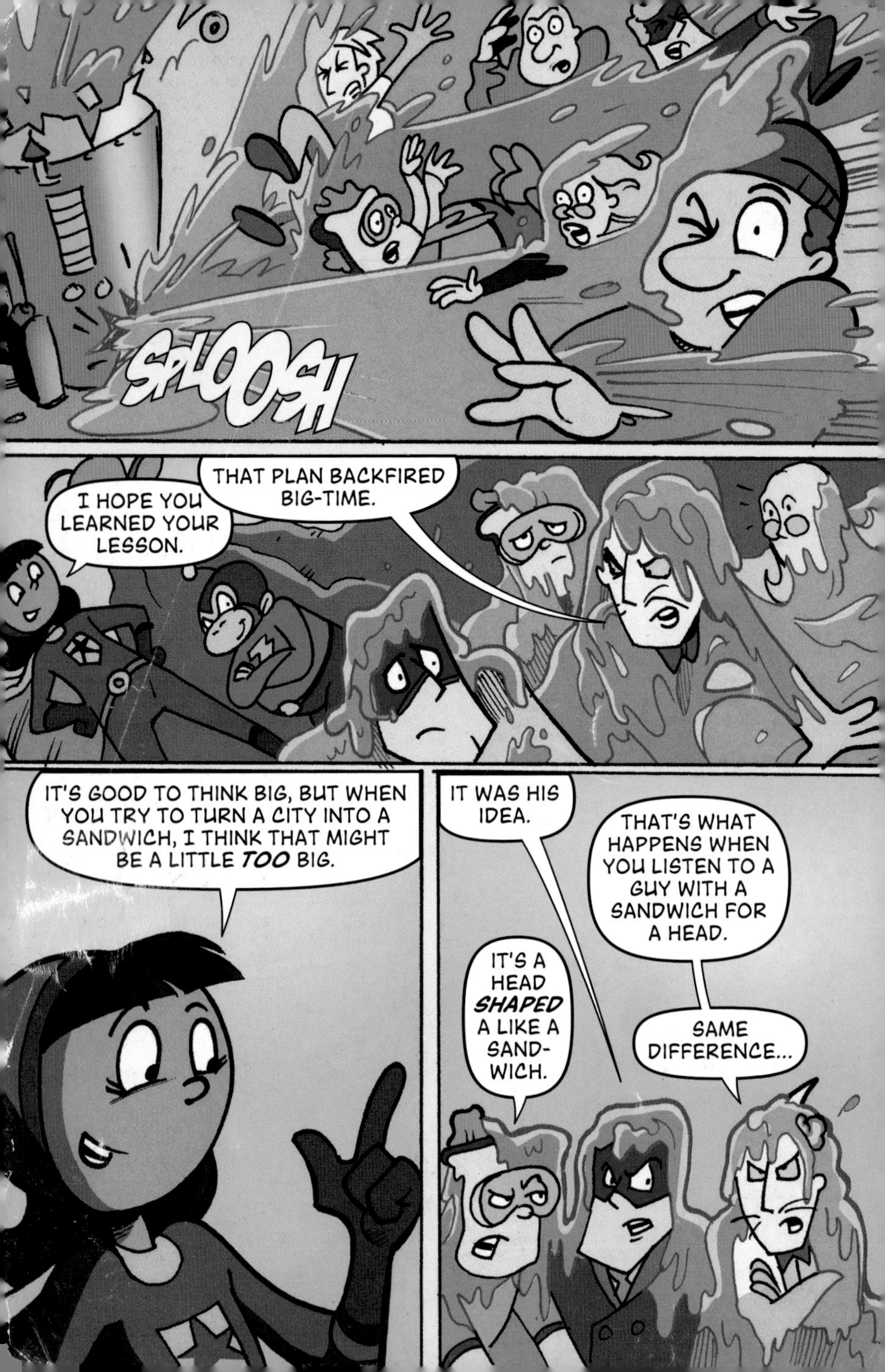
SPLOOSH
I HOPE YOU LEARNED YOUR LESSON.
THAT PLAN BACKFIRED BIG-TIME.
IT'S GOOD TO THINK BIG, BUT WHEN YOU TRY TO TURN A CITY INTO A SANDWICH, I THINK THAT MIGHT BE A LITTLE *TOO* BIG.
IT WAS HIS IDEA.
THAT'S WHAT HAPPENS WHEN YOU LISTEN TO A GUY WITH A SANDWICH FOR A HEAD.
IT'S A HEAD *SHAPED* A LIKE A SAND-WICH.
SAME DIFFERENCE...

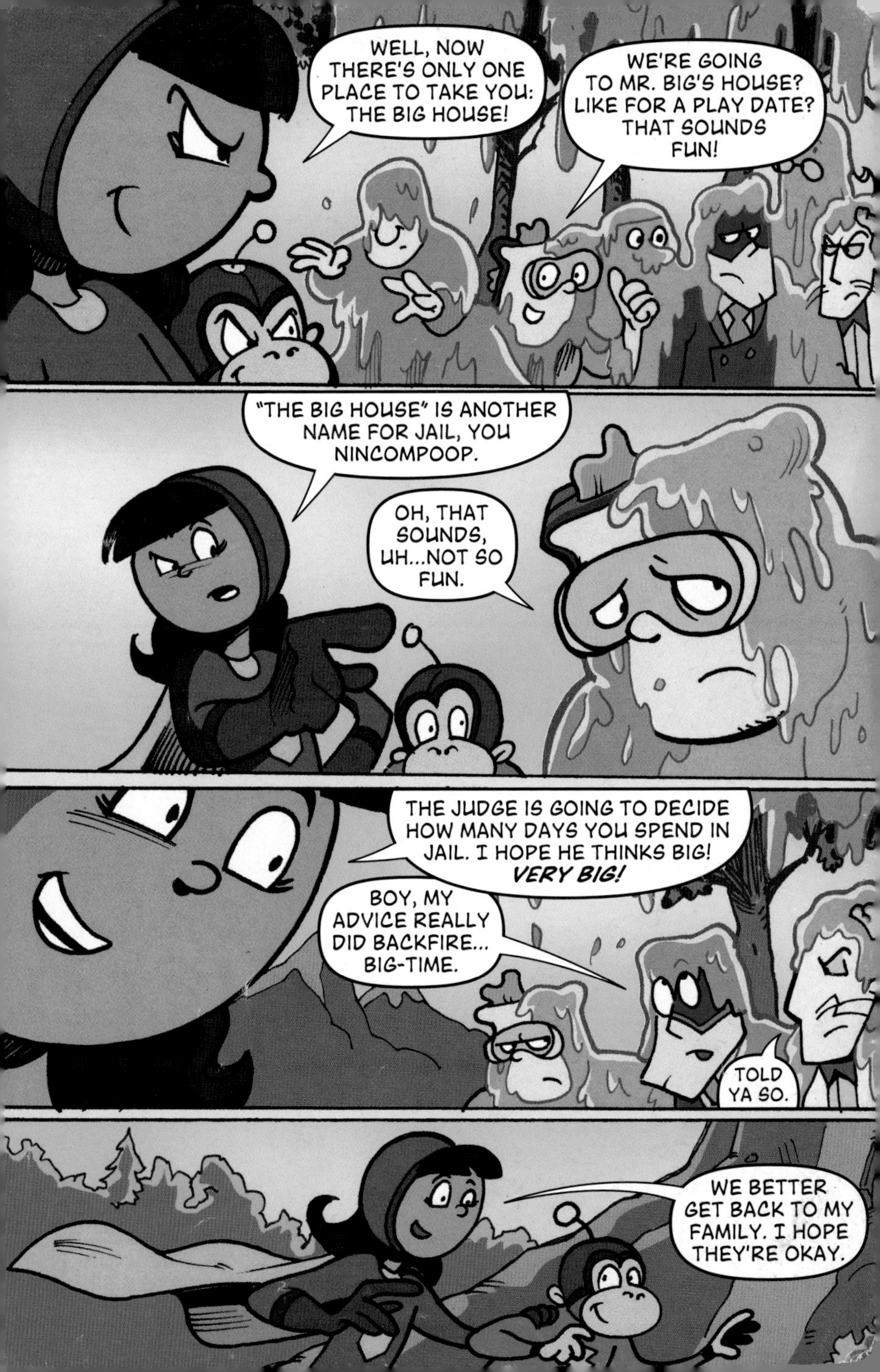
WELL, NOW THERE'S ONLY ONE PLACE TO TAKE YOU: THE BIG HOUSE!
WE'RE GOING TO MR. BIG'S HOUSE? LIKE FOR A PLAY DATE? THAT SOUNDS FUN!
"THE BIG HOUSE" IS ANOTHER NAME FOR JAIL, YOU NINCOMPOOP.
OH, THAT SOUNDS, UH...NOT SO FUN.
THE JUDGE IS GOING TO DECIDE HOW MANY DAYS YOU SPEND IN JAIL. I HOPE HE THINKS BIG! VERY BIG!
BOY, MY ADVICE REALLY DID BACKFIRE... BIG-TIME.
TOLD YA SO.
WE BETTER GET BACK TO MY FAMILY. I HOPE THEY'RE OKAY.

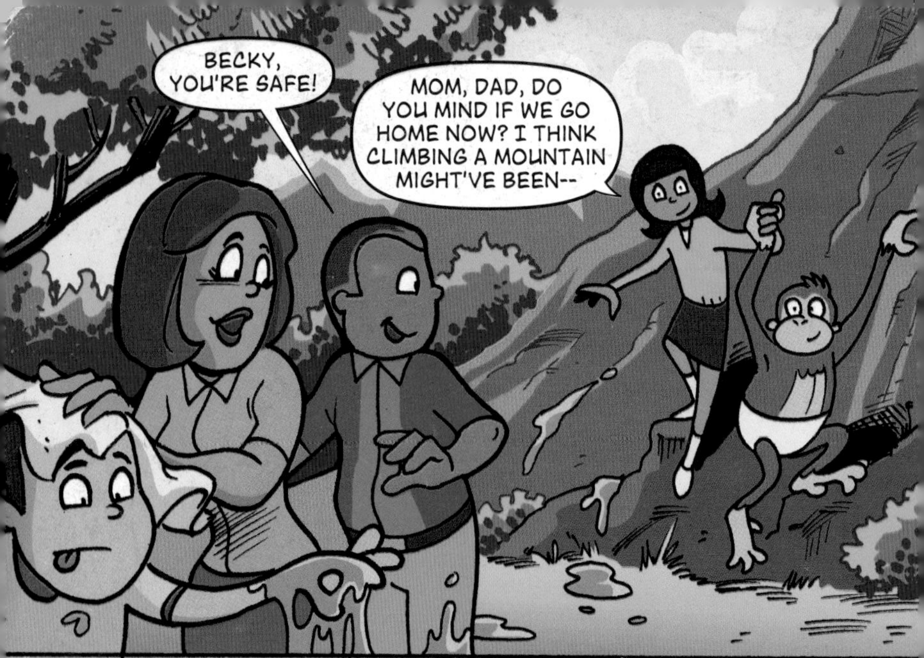
BECKY, YOU'RE SAFE!
MOM, DAD, DO YOU MIND IF WE GO HOME NOW? I THINK CLIMBING A MOUNTAIN MIGHT'VE BEEN--

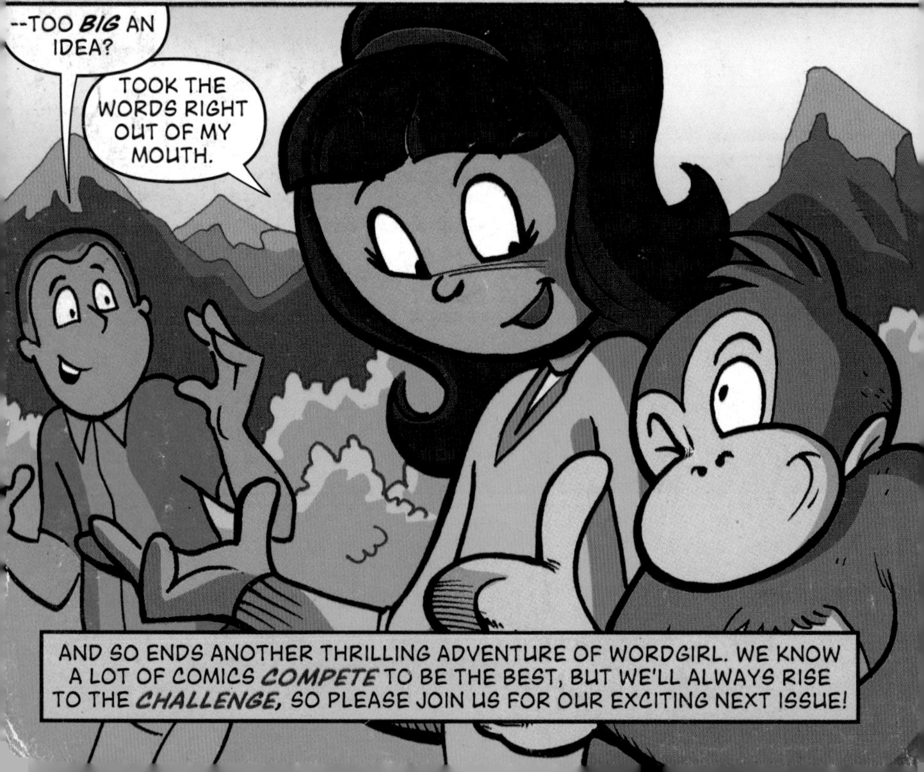
--TOO *BIG* AN IDEA?
TOOK THE WORDS RIGHT OUT OF MY MOUTH.
AND SO ENDS ANOTHER THRILLING ADVENTURE OF WORDGIRL. WE KNOW A LOT OF COMICS *COMPETE* TO BE THE BEST, BUT WE'LL ALWAYS RISE TO THE *CHALLENGE,* SO PLEASE JOIN US FOR OUR EXCITING NEXT ISSUE!

GLOSSARY

Yearn [yurn]
To have a strong desire or longing.

Oblivious [uh-bliv-ee-uh's]
Unmindful. Forgetful. Lacking active knowledge or awareness.

Promotion [pruh-moh-shuh'n]
Advancement in rank or position.

Resident [rez-i-duh'nt]
A person who lives in a particular place.

Pursuit [per-soot]
The act of chasing or following. An effort to secure or attain.

Import [im-pohrt]
To bring in, usually merchandise, commodities, or workers, from a foreign country for use.

Pickled [pik-uh'ld]
Preserved or seeped in brine or other liquid.

Paprika [pa-pree-kuh]
A red, powdery condiment derived from dried, ripe, sweet peppers.

Desperately [des-per-it-ly]
Reckless or dangerous because of despair or urgency.

Compete [kuh'm-peet]
To work or play to gain or win something over others who are trying to do the same.

Challenge [chal-inj]
A call to take part in a contest or competition.

Invention [in-ven-shuh'n]
Something new that was created using one's imagination.

Brilliant [bril-yuh'nt]
Shining brightly. Smart. Intelligent.

Positive [poz-i-tiv]
Emphasizing what is good or beneficial; constructive.

Repetitive [ri-pet-i-tiv]
The act of repeating an excessive amount. Unnecessary or tiresome.

Ridiculous [ri-dik-yuh-luh's]
Causing or worthy of ridicule. Absurd. Laughable.

Tangy [tang-ee]
Having a strong, pleasantly sharp flavor or smell.

Destined [des-tind]
Appointed or predetermined to be or do something.

Condiment [kon-duh-muh'nt]
Something used to give a flavor to a food, as mustard, ketchup, salt, or spices.

Backfire [bak-fahy-uh'r]
To bring a result opposite to that which was planned or expected.